VOL. 1, NO. 1   **WINTER 2017/2018**

FEATURES

STORIES

Getting Away, by Alan Orloff 3
Fairy Tales, by Art Taylor .11
Eb and Flo, by Josh Pachter .31
Crazy Cat Lady, by Barb Goffman 39
A Pie to Die For, by Meg Opperman 51
Murder at Madame Tussaud's, by Dan Andriacco. 56
Rooster Creek, by John M. Floyd 74
Don't Bank on It, by Jack Halliday 94
Dixie Quickies, by Michael Bracken 97
Flight to the Flirty Flamingo, by Kaye George 111

CLASSIC REPRINT DEPARTMENT

The Italian Tile Mystery, by James Holding. 117
Beside a Flowering Wall, by Fletcher Flora 138

POETRY

Black Cat Mystery Magazine #1 is copyright © 2017 by Wildside Press LLC. All rights reserved. Published by Wildside Press LLC, 9710 Traville Gateway Dr. #234, Rockville, MD 20850 USA. Visit us online at wildsidepress.com.

THE CAT'S PERCH

Welcome to the premiere issue of *Black Cat Mystery Magazine!*

When we decided to launch a companion mystery magazine to go with *Sherlock Holmes Mystery Magazine*, we took a long look at the current state of the mystery field, considering niches that aren't adequately served. Hardboiled? Cozy? Noir? Crime? Private eye? Suspense? Thriller? Something else?

Then, without warning, the largest mystery magazine publisher in the country cut both of its magazines back to six double issues per year. Yes, they will still be publishing about the same amount of fiction, overall, if you go by word count. But larger issues will allow for more novelets and novellas (which previously only ran in their two-per-year double-issues), and that means fewer stories published overall. And a regular contributor will find far fewer slots available.

With that in mind, we decided to concentrate on publishing short stories in *BCMM*. We will run longer works, of course, if we love them. But this is going to be primarily a home for short fiction. And, just as we publish new stories, we will also celebrate the field's past with the occasional classic reprint. (There are two in this issue.)

And as to genre...? Hardboiled? Cozy? Noir? Crime? Private eye? Suspense? Thriller?

We say—*Yes to all!*

We simply call them "Mystery." We won't shy away from intense, dark fiction that makes the hair on the back of your neck stand on end. Just as we won't turn down the next amateur detective in the finest Agatha Christie tradition. Storytelling matters most.

Read our first issue, and you'll know why there isn't another magazine like *Black Cat* out there. You're in for quite a ride—and it's only beginning!

—John & Carla

Staff

PUBLISHER

John Gregory Betancourt

EDITORS

John Gregory Betancourt
Carla Coupe

WILDSIDE PRESS SUBSCRIPTION SERVICES

Carla Coupe

PRODUCTION TEAM

Steve Coupe
Shawn Garrett
Ben Geyer
Helen McGee
Karl Würf

GETTING AWAY
Alan Orloff

The man previously known as Eddie "Light Touch" Elkins leaned forward and picked up the passport I'd just given him. Opened it. Read the name next to his picture.

"Jonathan Wells. Jonathan Wells. Jonathan Wells." He rolled the name along his tongue and swished it around his mouth. "Jonathan Freaking Wells. I like it. I really do."

I nodded, smiling.

Elkins/Wells held the passport to his face and squinted, turning it this way and that, examining it from every angle, as if evaluating one of the diamonds he'd just stolen. After intense scrutiny, he closed his eyes and hefted it a few times, his hands acting like a very delicate scale.

His eyes popped open. "Perfect. Just perfect."

My smile grew. Another satisfied customer. I provided unique travel and relocation services to a niche clientele. Wealthy criminals looking to hide, for life.

"Here's the rest." I slid a driver's license across the desk, along with a social security card, some credit cards, a birth certificate—all belonging to the newly-born Jonathan Wells. He picked up those documents and admired them, too. As he inspected each one, his grin grew wider, until it seemed to cover half his doughy face. "You do great work. My buddy was right."

"Thank you." Although I didn't actually do the document work myself—I farmed it out to a highly skilled forger—it was nice to be appreciated just the same, especially since my business was generated exclusively through word-of-mouth.

His eyes narrowed. "They look great. But will they work?"

"I've been doing this for more than twenty years. No complaints so far." I sat a little taller. "In addition to the documents themselves, I've created some personal history for Mr. Wells, a paper and electronic trail. Credit card purchases, cable installation, voter registration, bank accounts, gmail account, and the like. I've used a series of post office boxes and dummy addresses that I keep expressly for this purpose. If anyone looks into Jonathan Wells's past, they'll find a trail that indicates you weren't just born … today."

"Sounds thorough."

"It is." At any time, I might have eight or ten phony identities "living" phony lives in cyberspace. I didn't make their fake bios too elaborate, leaving just enough of a footprint to get my clients out of the country with a minimum of risk, should someone check into their past. In my business, details were the difference between life and death.

I handed Wells an empty manila envelope, and he stuffed the documents inside. "So what's the plan?" he asked. "Italy? France? Spain?"

Wells had requested refuge in Europe, and I didn't have any trouble obliging him. "Italy. Tuscany, to be exact. Through my contacts I've arranged a very nice, very secluded villa. Eight million dollars goes a long way." The bigger the budget, the easier to satisfy a client's wish, but I had to be careful not to go overboard. Too much glitz brought unwanted attention.

"Terrific. I've always wanted to retire to Italy. I've heard Italian women are very … affectionate."

"Your dream is now a reality. Many people would kill to live there, myself included." I filled him in on all the details, answered his questions, and told him not to worry, everything would go like clockwork. It always did. "Remember, if you have any problems, get in touch with my contact in Tuscany, Aldo. He's very well-connected and extremely loyal. He'll fix whatever needs fixing."

Wells tucked the envelope with his new life under his arm, cocked his head to the side. "One last question. How do I know you won't double-cross me somehow?"

"Like I said, I've been doing this for twenty-some years. If I started double-crossing my clients, I wouldn't have a business anymore, would I?"

"Guess not. So when—"

I held up my hand. "Not that I don't have every reason in the world to trust you, but I feel compelled to let you know that you can't double-cross me, either. Like taking care of me so I could never divulge your secret. I haven't told my guy in Italian Customs your name yet— I'll wait until I've confirmed that you've boarded your flight. And, if something untoward should ever happen to me, I've left instructions— and a list of my clients' aliases and other incriminating information— with a dear friend who will take it to the authorities." I smiled. "Can't be too careful, right?"

Wells glared at me, then broke out his own smile. "Sure thing. No worries on my end."

"Excellent."

We both rose. He extended his hand and I took it, pumped it a couple of times. "Good luck, Mr. Wells. Good luck."

The bell over the door to my tiny storefront jangled, and my client was gone. He'd be totally gone in another few days when he completed his transformation into Jonathan Wells's skin.

I leaned back in my worn leather swivel chair and took stock of my life.

Ever since college, I'd run a travel agency, Lloyd Birnbaum Travel, a one-man specialty shop. The business had changed drastically in that span, especially once the Internet arrived in every home, enabling everyone to be a travel agent. Now, most people booked their own trips and relied on sites like TripAdvisor, Vacation Genie, and Rate-MyPlace to steer them to the best spots, provide them with the most useful travel tips. Travel agents were a dying breed.

Luckily, I saw where things were headed early on, and I was eager to adapt. So when an acquaintance of mine wanted to ditch his life here in the U.S. and start fresh abroad, he came to me. I knew a guy who knew a guy who knew a guy who could provide a new identity, top to bottom, A to Z. I embraced the role of planner, organizer, coordinator. Relocation *counselor*.

That first client told his friends. And they told their friends, and my sideline business boomed.

Over the years, I carefully cultivated an extensive network of international contacts—border patrol officers, customs officials, real estate agents, local and regional bureaucrats—all willing to assist me for a price. I used my contacts and my experience to book my clients' travel and get them set up in a foreign locale.

I knew which countries were most hospitable to fugitives. I knew which government officials would look the other way. I knew which communities would welcome new neighbors with *nouveau* money, regardless of how it was obtained. I also knew which places to avoid.

My utter discretion and attention to detail fostered my success. I got paid to cover everyone's tracks, and I did a damn good job of it.

Some travel agents catered to high rollers. Others specialized in families.

I helped criminals who wanted to disappear and had the means to do so in style. I was the best at what I did.

But after three decades in the travel biz, I'd grown weary. Time to retire.

I picked up a grip strengthener and leaned back in my chair. As I did my daily exercises—twenty squeezes, each hand—I glanced around at the Nineties-era travel posters hanging on the wall. I'd been looking at them for decades, imagining myself visiting those exotic places, carefree. Ironically, I'd never found the time to actually *go* on spectacular vacations. Too busy working.

I'd saved a decent amount of money over the years, living within my means. Of course, I didn't have the money most of my clients did, not by a long shot, but I had enough to get started. It would be nice to spread my wings a little and explore the wide world.

Experience what my clients have been experiencing.

I finished my grip exercises and fed Elkins's file through the shredder. *Goodbye, Eddie.* I had a few things to take care of before I closed up shop for good. Attention to detail was so important in my line of work.

* * * *

Ryan Marsteller ran a graphic design firm and like me, he'd used his special skills to develop his own sideline business. Document forger *extraordinaire*. He was a young, string-bean-of-a-kid who reminded me of a praying mantis: angular limbs given to herky, jerky movements, and beady unblinking eyes.

Marsteller worked out of an extra bedroom in his apartment, and we sat across the desk from each other while we conducted a little of that extracurricular business.

"Going on a trip, huh? Nice, nice." He stared at me a beat, then handed me two packages. "There you go. Everything you wanted, Lloyd. Or should I say Thomas?"

I opened one of the packages and fished out the passport. The name Thomas Jensen next to a picture of me. As usual, Marsteller's work was flawless. I sorted through the other documents and ID cards. All top notch. All with my new Jensen identity.

"So what do you think?" Marsteller asked.

"Very nice."

His face broke into a grin, as if he was four and his mother just complimented his coloring. Sometimes I thought he did this more for the kudos and atta-boys than for the money. "Thanks. I take great pride in my work. And in my confidentiality. I can be trusted, and that means something these days, you know?"

"I couldn't agree more," I said.

"How long will you be gone?"

I shrugged. Even if I knew the specifics, it was none of Marsteller's concern. I opened the other package and removed the passport. Examined it. A very attractive brunette stared back at me. Name: Sarah Jensen.

Marsteller leaned over the desk and gawked at her picture, too. "Quite a looker. She your daughter?"

I shook my head but didn't say anything. She was more than twenty years my junior.

"Oh, ho. I get it. Wife, huh?"

I kept quiet.

He grinned, then bobbed his head. "Nice. Very nice. You're a lucky man."

I *was* a lucky man. And I'd do whatever necessary to keep my luck running good. I took an envelope from my jacket pocket and tossed it on the desk.

Marsteller flashed me his silly grin again as he picked it up. Leafed through the stack of Benjamins. I guessed he liked the money, too. "Pleasure doing business with you. As always."

I opened my passport and looked at it again. Squinted at the picture. Chewed on my lip. "Huh."

"What?" Marsteller asked. "What's wrong?"

"Well, not to complain, but I noticed one small blemish. On my photo."

A frowning Marsteller reached across the desk and grabbed my passport. Examined it closely. "I don't see anything wrong."

"Really? I could have sworn …" I got up and went around behind him, so I could look over his shoulder. I pointed to my picture. "There, on the cheek."

Marsteller picked up a loupe and hunched over the passport.

I pulled a garrote out of my jacket pocket, wrapped the piano wire around his throat from behind, and tightened, tightened, *tightened*.

Seated as he was, Marsteller didn't have a chance. He gave it his best effort, though, bucking and clawing, but after a minute, he slumped over, dead.

I slipped my passport out from under his head, reclaimed my envelope with the cash, and checked his apartment, just to make sure there weren't any traces of me or records of business we'd done over the years. I gathered anything that might remotely connect us, and took a few minutes to remove the hard drive from his desktop computer. I found two additional laptops, a box of thumbdrives and memory cards, and three portable drives. I crammed all this stuff into an old cardboard box.

Before I left Marsteller's, I called a guy who knew a guy who specialized in delicate clean-up operations. Gave him the address and details, then picked up the box and hit the road.

Marsteller had been the only one to know my new identity.

* * * *

Annette and I sat at her small kitchen table, her hands cradled around a mug of hot tea. I wasn't sure what I'd done to deserve the likes of her, but I'd never sought that answer, afraid I would somehow spoil the magic. I'd been seeing her for two years now, and when I came over, we usually hit the bedroom as soon as I walked through the door. Today, I had something I wanted to discuss first.

"So, what is it?" Her eyes twinkled. "What's so important?"

I'd waited while she made tea, about to burst with the good news, but now that I had her attention, I hesitated, knowing my life was about to change. In a big way. I took a deep breath and placed her passport on the table. "Will you be my wife?"

Annette's twinkling eyes grew large, and she carefully opened the passport, as if something might come jumping out from between the pages. She read the name, first to herself, then aloud. "Sarah Jensen? I'm not sure I understand."

I pulled out my passport and opened it to my picture. "I'm Thomas Jensen. Your husband-to-be."

Annette looked from me to the passport and back to me. The spark in her eyes dimmed.

"Well? Will you be my wife?"

She sighed. "I'm already married, Lloyd. I don't think Jay would approve."

"You love me. We'll have a new life together."

She stared at me and I saw confusion, then fright. "You're serious?"

"We can blow this popsicle stand, as they say." I tapped my new passport. "You are now the lovely Sarah Jensen, wife of Thomas Jensen. We'll move away. You and me. A fresh start."

"But, Lloyd …"

"How does Europe sound? If that seems too boring, what about the South Pacific? I know you like palm trees."

"We talked about this. I can't just take off." Her words spilled out fast.

"I know you love me. Leave him. Now's our chance. For happiness."

She stared at the passport, glanced up, eyes shimmering. "I do care about you. But …"

"What?" I swallowed.

"We had a great time, Lloyd. And you're a sweet guy. But there's Jay. And my job. And my friends. And … and a thousand other things."

"Am I too old?"

She didn't answer, just offered a sad smile. I crunched the numbers in my head. When I was seventy-five, she'd barely be fifty. The older I got, the larger the chasm would grow. Time had a weird way of dilating with age.

She put her hand on top of mine. "This has been fun. Really. But I can't run away with you."

"You could. If you wanted to." My pulse raced.

Annette pushed the passport across the table. "I'm flattered." She pulled her hand back and took a long sip of tea, eying me over the mug's rim. "And I'm sorry."

I stuffed the two passports into my right jacket pocket, then removed the garrote from the left. "I'm sorry, too."

* * * *

Back in my office, I fed Sarah Jensen's passport through the shredder. Then I made travel arrangements for Thomas Jensen, cleaned out the petty cash drawer, packed the few things of any value, and locked the front door for the last time.

Walked away without even a backward glance.

After eating an early dinner at the local Chinese restaurant, I returned to my apartment and pulled out my dog-eared Moleskin journal. Found a blank page and jotted down a few notes from the vacation itinerary I'd been working up in my head.

The counterfeiter formerly known as Keith Pritzkin, now William Southwick, lived along the beach in Nice, France. I heard Nice was nice.

The mob lawyer formerly known as Tony Coretti, now Elliot Cor-man, lived three miles outside of Barcelona. Spain was beautiful, I'd read.

The white-collar criminal formerly known as Harvey Katz, now Roger Robbins, lived in a cottage in Kent, England. The English countryside was supposed to be quite charming.

I knew I could count on my local contacts for help with logistics, muscle, and cover-up—I'd been very generous in my payouts over the years. I'd be able to knock off my former clients and steal their fortunes. With a little luck, I could access their bank and investment accounts using their personal data—data I'd fabricated for their new identities.

And no one would miss them.

After all, they weren't even real men. I'd created them. I could erase them.

When I finished my sightseeing tour and was ready to settle down, I'd call my loyal friend Aldo to help me move into that dreamy Tuscan villa, soon to be the *former* home of Jonathan Wells.

I'd heard good things about Italian women, too.

I pulled an old Fodor's guide off the shelf and began reading about my upcoming trip of a lifetime.

✗

Alan Orloff has published seven novels, including *Diamonds For The Dead* (Agatha Award finalist). His short fiction has appeared in *Jewish Noir*, *Alfred Hitchcock's Mystery Magazine*, *Chesapeake Crimes: Storm Warning*, *Mystery Weekly*, *50 Shades Of Cabernet*, *Noir At The Salad Bar*, and *Windward: Best New England Crime Stories 2016*. www.alanorloff.com

FAIRY TALES
Art Taylor

Once, William Washington hadn't minded the kids who walked through his neighborhood after school. But when classes started up this latest fall, he decided he didn't care much for a good many of them.

From his porch each afternoon, he watched the far end of the street, the doors bursting open at the new high school, slick glass windows glinting like a new Cadillac, and the kids pouring out in all directions. Kids from William's own neighborhood headed toward the rowhouses that lined street after street or toward the basketball court half-a-block over, regularly a crowd there—children whose families he knew, children he'd watched grow up. He didn't mind these kids, felt protective of them.

But the others, those headed through William's neighborhood to homes further west … wasn't there something about the attitude they carried with them? The way they walked? And the where too—not on the sidewalk but right down the middle of the road sometimes, like they expected the cars to curve around them? Even on the sidewalk, they just stood there—in the way. *Loitering*, William thought, and *idleness* and not just that but *entitlement*—that was the word. All of it rubbed him wrong, and seemed to him like the attitude had turned worse lately.

Day after day of it, and finally William hoisted himself up from his rocker, went into the kitchen, and picked up the phone.

"9-1-1. What is your emergency?"

"Yes, ma'am," he said. "Suspicious folks out on the street."

"And your location?"

"Cedar. Just off Ninth."

"And you say someone is doing something suspicious. What is this person doing?"

"People. More than one. Boys."

"And what are these boys doing?"

"They walking."

"Walking, sir?"

"Most of 'em. One have a skateboard."

The woman on the other end didn't say anything. William stretched the phone cord through the hallway so he could look out the window. There they stood, same as before. The skateboarder rolled slightly back and forth.

"Skateboarding," she said finally. "Can you describe what makes them suspicious to you?"

Many things, William could've told her.

"Don't live here," he said instead. "Don't seem like they visiting nobody. Just wandering around. Maybe they up to trouble."

"So you don't recognize them?"

"Dangerous. Cars having to stop and go around 'em."

"And your name, sir?"

He paused. He wasn't sure why the woman asked that. He felt certain she already had his name, this day of caller ID.

"I'm with the neighborhood watch. More than fifty year of it," he said. "Full-time now."

A pause on the end of the line. He started to count to ten in his head, then caught himself wondering if the woman was counting to ten too.

"I'll pass the report along to the proper authorities," she said, about the time William reached nine.

He didn't like the way she said *proper*, but he let it go. Went back to the front porch and settled into his seat to see what happened next.

The boys stood there still, no rush to get through the neighborhood, that same one skateboarding back and forth. Several times, cars curved past them, beeped the horn. Didn't seem to faze them.

"See the sidewalk," William called out after awhile. "You could use it."

One of the boys laughed. Another of them waved. Or maybe he was giving the finger. William's eyesight had faded a little.

Either way, no one moved.

William got up again, went to the kitchen.

"What is your emergency?"

"Been 15 minutes," he said. "No police."

It was a different woman, he could tell, but he figured they had a record.

"Sir?"

"I done called before, but no one come to help. Can you explain that?"

"What is your emergency?"

"Dangerous for everybody."

"You said danger, sir. Is your life being threatened?"

He looked at the clock on his stove. It was broken and flashed the same time again and again. 12:00, 12:00, 12:00. Was it trying to blink noon or midnight? William had wondered sometimes which it would be.

"Guess that depend on what you mean by *life*," he said. "What you mean by *your*."

And by *threatened* too, he thought a few seconds later, but by then, he'd hung up.

* * * *

It was three weeks before William told anyone about his 9-1-1 calls. Henry, a fellow retiree and sometime drinking buddy, stopped by one afternoon unannounced, and William felt like it was a sign to share.

Henry gave a little laugh after he heard. "How many times have you called them?"

"Forty-seven," William said. "A bunch of groups passing here every day. All of 'em out of place."

"The police haven't shown up yet?"

"Cruised through. No lights. Never stopped, except …."

"Except what?"

William shifted in his seat. "Except to step up here once, tell me to stop calling in 'false reports.'"

"But you call back anyway?"

"Started keeping a timesheet." He pointed to a notebook on the small table between Henry's chair and his own, then picked up a handset. "Bought a cordless phone too, save myself some walking."

Henry snorted. "Seems like that bit of exercise might've been the only useful thing about this nonsense."

"Upper arm workout now." William flexed a muscle. "Lifting the phone so many times a day."

"You already had that with your beers." Henry tipped up his own bottle to illustrate.

School had let out as they talked. William could see movement over in the distance—crowds of kids beginning to emerge from the front doors, fanning out, an exodus. Ahead of the larger pack, a tall, lanky boy skateboarded past, again right down the middle of the street—earbuds stuffed in each ear, his stringy hair flopping. A car honked, swerved, but the boy didn't seem to notice.

William picked up the phone. "Forty-eight," he told Henry as he dialed the number. After he made his report, he logged the call on his sheet.

"I've seen our kids doing the same things," Henry said after William had hung up. "They skateboard in the street sometimes, they stand around in big groups, killing time, messing around. You call the cops on them too?"

William thought about that for a minute—or pretended to. He'd already thought it through pretty well. *Our* kids, his neighbors' children—children he and his wife had helped raise in some way, a couple of generations of them now. William had taught some of them how to garden, holding their own hands in his as they eased seeds into the ground or watered new sprouts. Sometimes they kept up with it. Sometimes they wandered.

He and Sarah had raised two children themselves, grown now, grown up good he liked to think.

"You know what used to rile Sarah?" William said. "Sitting at a stoplight—or hell, just sitting here on the porch looking at the intersection there—and seeing some driver thump a cigarette into the street. 'Would they do that in they own yard?' she used to ask. And I'd say, 'Who know? They might,' and she'd say, 'I doubt it,'' and then I ask, 'Would it make it better if they did?'"

"And would it?" Henry asked.

"Still an eyesore in they own yard. But more of a right."

"But this isn't their yard, it's the street. Belongs to everybody."

William drank his beer, saw another group of kids lingering in front of the house, started to pick up the phone, then didn't.

"Why they need to stop here anyway? Why here?"

"A taste of danger. A little bit of the *other*." Henry put some insistence behind the word.

"The other what?"

"Any *other*." Same insistence. "Some other place, some different place. Like when we used to go out into the woods when we were kids, back when there were woods way out there. This here, this is the wilderness for them, the jungle."

"The jungle?"

"Like those idiots wanted to go to 'Nam while the rest of us knew better. While we wanted to go anywhere but."

William looked at the street in front of him, his neighborhood for nearly half a century now. Rowhouses lined each side of the road, some with small porches like his, others just with stoops and iron railings. He thought about that time, back in the early '90s, when things had taken a turn for the worse—the crack years. Dealers hanging around on the corners, trash left in the street, the whole place feeling tired and run-down. William had been making calls then too—fast as he was making them now. Different kids, different complaints, and really no more response back then either.

But these days … a change had come. The drug trade had moved on, the neighborhood had been cleaned up. Some of the new owners had painted their houses, put little patches of flowers out front, taken some pride in the place. Just here and there, but it was spreading. The kids who lived here—*our* kids, like Henry had called them—had cleaned up too, most of them.

"This ain't 'Nam, you know that," William said. "Maybe once upon a time, but not today."

The two of them watched the street some more. Henry finished his beer, opened another one.

"Okay, try this," he said. "Your 'once upon a time' there, like you said. These kids, they're like a bunch of Little Red Riding Hoods. Their folks tell them what not to do. Don't go down this street, don't talk to strangers, come right home after school. But they have their own minds, see. So here they come, picture of innocence—dumb, right? But not bad, no, not that—just testing the limits, dipping a toe into that wilderness I was talking about and thinking that it's fine, they're good people, what could go wrong? And after a while, they think not only is the wilderness okay but that it's theirs to use however they want."

Entitlement—that was the word again, the way they thought.

William and Henry had gone in different directions after Vietnam. William had settled into a job mowing and trimming for a big company that did groundskeeping for strip malls, married the woman who did the accounting, ended up opening his own landscaping business, raised those two children who'd long since moved on to other things—a son in Texas now, a daughter in Chicago he didn't talk to as much as he would've liked, each of them half-a-country away, drifting further now that their mother wasn't around anymore to hold them close.

Meanwhile, Henry had gone to college and then grad school, become an English teacher. He'd never married, said more than once that he lived for his books—and that was sure clear sometimes. But he didn't lord that education over anyone. He was easy to sit with, to talk to over a beer.

"Red Riding Hood," said William. "All that talk about hoodies, but them *other* kids like to wear them too."

Black kids, white kids—matching Henry's *other* with his own.

About that time, a couple of students from the school strolled past—a boy and a girl, both wearing hoodies, and the girl's red, like the conversation had conjured them up.

They were talking, words William couldn't make out, then the boy bumped his side into the girl—hard, William thought, and he started to call out to them—but just as suddenly they were holding hands.

The boy was clearly from that other neighborhood further east, but William recognized the girl from just down his own block, which put a twist on everything Henry had been saying about Little Red sneaking a toe into the wilderness. Just a girl, innocent sure, that age, but she'd grown up in this place Henry called jungle. So who was wandering where? Who was testing what? William couldn't tell which of them had reached out for the other's hand first.

"Fairy tales, they not as simple as you putting them," William said. "But some sense there, I guess."

Henry grunted. "Glad to help," he said. "But remember. That means you're the big bad wolf, right? And me too. And all of us here."

Big bad wolf, William thought, as the couple turned a corner.

It seemed clear Henry hadn't noticed them at all.

* * * *

William saw the same couple walking again the next day when he sat alone on the porch—the girl in her bright red hoodie, the boy's a silvery gray.

They were a new couple, William felt sure of it now, new to whatever was happening between them. Something about the body language, how the girl leaned into the boy with one step and then away from him with another. Something innocent in all that, same as Henry had said—all of it becoming clearer. Some testing of things for both of them, some crossing of lines.

William watched the girl shift closer to the boy and then drift away. She wasn't yet comfortable with him, William felt that too—Little Red realizing she'd wandered too wide.

Reading too much into it probably, after all that talk of Henry's.

At least the boy kept on the sidewalk, there was that.

Near William's house, the boy stopped and the girl stopped with him. He tugged at her sleeve, and she turned around toward him. Time to make his move, he pulled her into a kiss. Hesitant at first, on the girl's part at least, then not so much on the boy's.

Necking, that's what they'd called it in William's day. He couldn't remember what his own boys had called it. Had no idea what they called it now. Back then, necking wasn't something you did in public, at least not like this and not with ….

He thought again about that phrase *crossing lines*.

More kids passed by. A few wide eyes here and there, some giggling. It didn't seem to slow the couple down. The boy was insistent. The neighborhood kids—*our* kids, William thought again—paid less mind, rolled their eyes, shook their heads, turned back to their own friends. Whoops and shouts at the basketball court, but William realized it was part of the game, nothing to do with what was unfolding in front of him.

Almost directly across the street, a young woman sat on her own porch. Emma was her name. She babysat her niece and nephew during the day while the children's mother worked. Lived with the family too. Emma and William had talked sometimes, and he'd tried to help her tend a little flowerbed through the hottest parts of the summer. Her eyes met William's, and William was glad the niece and nephew were still napping.

It wasn't just the public part of it but the panting and pawing—and there was plenty of that suddenly. William didn't know what this girl's parents might've thought, but he knew he wouldn't have wanted his own daughter touched that way, especially by a boy like that.

"You got a house you can take that to?" he called out.

The girl's face spun around quick, pulling away from the boy. She hadn't known William was there, that was clear. He searched her expression for some sign of gratitude but saw only panic and confusion. A girl in a bad place, in too deep. He was glad he'd spoken up.

The boy stared straight ahead, still in position for the kissing that had stopped. Slowly he turned his head William's way, and William could see anger curving around the set of his jaw.

"Excuse me," the boy said—the tone clear that he wasn't asking to be excused.

William leaned forward so they could see him better. "Our street ain't your bedroom." *And that girl not yours to bed*, that thought crossed his mind too.

"*Your* street?"

"My house, my view." He gave a broad sweep with his arm. "Our view. Everybody right now, seem like."

Across the street, Emma nodded lightly.

"No charge to watch," said the boy, grinning.

"No choice not to."

"Just keep it in your pants, old man," the boy said, and his voice growled, became deeper—older than William would've expected. The grin had disappeared.

"I'm telling you to keep it in yours," William said, bristling as much at the *old man* as at the boy's tone.

The boy still held the girl, but she had pulled away from him more, arching her back to put more distance between their faces. She whispered something to him, tried to pull an arm free. The boy said something back, shook his head, tested out some tentative kisses one more time. William fought an urge to step down and free her himself.

Before he could, they'd settled back into it—the kisses more fervent now, more frantic, and the girl more willing it seemed. She did brush his hand away when he reached up inside the red hoodie, but when he moved that hand to cradle her rear end, she let it stay. The boy seemed to be putting on a show, and as they angled their heads around one another, he looked up at William, his eyes wide open, gleaming hatred.

William picked up the phone. He'd put 9-1-1 on speed-dial now—only one button to press instead of three.

"Girl getting molested on the street in front of my house," he said to the person who answered. "Better hurry. Big fellow, pretty aggressive. 'Bout to tear her shirt off."

This time he felt like the police might actually arrive.

This time they did.

* * * *

Even before the first car pulled up, William had known there would be repercussions. The boy angry and accusatory. The girl embarrassed and defensive. Across the street, Emma's niece and nephew had been wakened by the sirens, and she struggled to pull them away from the windows. Older kids gathered on the street to watch—the neighborhood kids and the other kids both—straining their necks, laughing, pointing toward the couple. Soon they were pointing toward William too, especially after the police turned their own attention his way.

"Do you know what you can get for making a false 9-1-1 call?" one of the policemen asked. Beefy fellow. "Up to $2500 in fines. Up to a year in jail. Maybe both."

"Can't help but worry," he told the officer. "Hard to tell *what* going on these days. So many *strangers* coming through this neighborhood, better to be safe than sorry."

"Strangers?" the officer said. He turned to look at the young couple, then back. William squinted at him, trying to recognize his features, wondering if he'd grown up in the neighborhood himself. The man was clearly not on William's side.

Through it all—his own explanations to the police, the girl protesting that she hadn't been attacked—the boy leveled his eyes in William's direction. Snake eyes, William thought. And then, no. Wolf eyes, that was it. Hungry when he'd been pawing and scratching at the girl. Little Red. Then cold and menacing toward William, vengeful-looking.

No surprise there, none at all. William steadied his own gaze back, watched the boy's sneer deepen, watched his shoulders roll under that gray hoodie.

Gray wolf, William thought—the look and the hoodie the boy wore. And then not gray but silver—something about the word's sharpness, the way it gleamed. *Silverwolf* and Little Red, predator and prey, just like he'd tell it to Henry later.

But that brought back Henry's other comments. Who was William himself in the middle of all this?

* * * *

"Trouble brewing," William said on the phone with Henry later that evening, after telling him about the newest twists on the tale. "I don't mean skateboarders. And I don't just mean boys grabbing ass in the street. It's attitude. It's … Ain't nobody taking me seriously about it, not even you. And now this policeman tell *me* that *I'm* the one got the problem?"

"There's a difference between *seeing* trouble and *seeking* it," Henry said. "A difference between trouble wandering down your street and you inviting it in."

"Way he groping her, coulda been a rape right there."

"Did you really believe that?" Henry asked.

"Boy look like an animal in heat," William said. "And you the one say this a jungle, a wilderness. Something needed taming. Somebody."

"Are you going to stop making calls?"

William thought about it. "I don't know."

"Well, you need to know. You need to take a good look at all this, at yourself."

William thought about that too, remembered the boy's eyes.

"We ain't the wolves," he said. "I ain't gonna let no sheep get taken in. Ain't gonna be a sheep myself."

* * * *

The boy—Silverwolf—returned the next day. Little Red too. And they weren't alone. Beards and goatees on some of their friends, kids he'd seen passing through at other times, and then some others, boys he recognized from the neighborhood right here, which he wouldn't want to tell Henry later. Several of them had that same cold look in their eyes—all except the girl, whose expression seemed guarded, even blank.

They stood near the same spot where the boy had been groping her the day before, stood in a little circle. A huddle it looked like, and from time to time one or another of them threw relentless glares in William's direction.

He sat in the same spot, same phone at his side, his hand on it. Twice now he'd almost dialed the number, and twice now he'd stopped, reminded of the officer's caution.

"You boys got something to say?" William hollered toward the little huddle.

Silverwolf stepped up. "Talking to my friends," he said. "Not to you."

"Seen you look my way," William said. "Figure you might be talking *'bout* me. Don't think I was wrong."

The boy shook his head. "Many things you might be wrong about, old man."

More huddling, more whispering—the phrase *old man* again, rankling William's nerves.

As the crowd slowly broke up, Silverwolf pulled Little Red toward him, dipped her into a kiss with one arm. She didn't seem to resist today, something yielding in her this time, submissive, helpless it seemed like, and William felt helpless himself.

Nothing wrong with William's eyesight this time. What happened next was clear. With the hand that wasn't dipping the girl, Silverwolf raised his middle finger and pointed it William's way.

* * * *

"Sarah," William called out a few hours later, a little after midnight—called out from somewhere deep in his sleep, a hoarse, urgent whisper. He woke to find himself sitting up, one arm reached out across the empty spot in the bed, shielding a wife who was no longer there. The children, he thought the same instant, his son and daughter upstairs. How would he get to them? And then came the slow realization that they weren't there either.

Then he recognized what had startled him awake: something moving against the side of the house.

William took a few deep breaths, counted to ten to calm himself, then strained to listen closer. Some kind of scratching? Something rubbing against the wall? He didn't know exactly how to describe the sound, couldn't quite place it.

Nothing good coming of it, that was for sure.

He pulled himself up out of the bed and started for the phone in the kitchen—picked it up and then stopped and looked at it, thought about the warning the policeman had given him, watched the clock on the stove blinking out its 12:00 again and again.

More movement from outside, something pushing against the house. Against the door?

No, just the walls, almost keeping beat with that blinking clock. No one trying to get in.

Not yet, at least.

After he returned the phone to its cradle, William went down the hall to the closet, felt the weight of his wife's jackets pushing against him as he reached toward the top shelf—so many jackets, she was always talking about the cold. He couldn't bring himself to get rid of them yet, the way they held the smell of her. He found the box he was looking for, pulled it down.

The gun was still there, the one from his service days. A little Colt Automatic. Back in the early to mid-'90s, he'd kept it in his bedside table, or in the kitchen, or sometimes in a little bag out on the porch. Easy access. But he'd put it away when things got better.

He hefted it in his hand. Didn't even know if it worked anymore, or if he'd know how to aim it right. Point and shoot, he thought. Then: just point. Because if it came to it, he only needed to scare whoever was out there, right?

He sat down on a chair in the hallway, the Colt on his lap. From there, he could see most of the first floor of the house: the front door, the streetlights shining through the window in the front parlor, the back window in the kitchen, shadows in the bedroom. With a brief turn, he could look in the bathroom too, but that window was small—too small for anyone to come through.

The gun in his lap reminded him of the first time he'd shot a man. Back in Vietnam. Guard duty one dark night, darker than tonight, moonless. But not motionless out there in that darkness half a world away, where every sound had seemed a threat. His ears had picked up the slightest rustle, and when one didn't sound just right ….

That night had been the first time he'd seen the enemy's face up close—up close and alive. Alive briefly, at least, and then not. And then faceless too.

Gook, he'd thought, as he'd killed him, and then thought that word many times afterwards too. And not just thought it but said it, time and again, even after the adrenaline and fear and anger had been tamped down.

He'd gotten a commendation for it. Service to his unit. Service to his country. Something like that.

Sometimes the past just faded away. Sometimes it felt like he was still right in the middle of it.

Outside now he heard a snuffling sound, and then a yelp, sudden and sharp, just as suddenly stifled. Or maybe it was a howl.

"Wolves," William said aloud. Then: "Wolf." Silverwolf. He'd known that all along.

Then, thinking about the scratching, rubbing, snuffling, he reconsidered. "Wrong story," he said then. "Hansel and Gretel." It gave him a little laugh, but then wrong story there as well. No brother and sister these two.

He felt the gun in his lap. Only one of them he'd have to scare off.

He waited to hear something more. When nothing came, he stepped to the kitchen, poured himself a couple of fingers' worth of Wild Turkey, then took his post again.

Long after the sounds stopped, he kept sitting in that chair, remembering the last time he'd sat like this. His wife had been back in the bedroom, and his children had been up in their own beds, and trouble had lurked outside, almost constantly, the dealers, the buyers. Neighborhood truly did feel like the jungle then, he'd have given Henry that—bad as 'Nam in its own way, and him ready to defend wife and children and home even more strongly than he'd fought for his country.

So much had changed. No wife, no drug deals, children grown and gone. And yet …

Probably an hour he sat there after whoever was outside had left—sat there, fingering the gun, rubbing his hand across it, sipping the bourbon, keeping watch over what was his, what little hadn't been eaten away by time, by everything.

* * * *

The next morning, he made an inspection of the small yard around him. Two beer bottles had been stuck neck down into a flowerbed in the back, a patch of the begonias had been trampled—on purpose or not, he wasn't sure. There was a condom slung across one of the back steps, a little stain on the lower step where it had dripped. A scrap of fabric clung to a nail sticking out of one of the risers.

William pulled the fabric loose from the nail. A couple of shades of red there, the darker shade looked like blood.

* * * *

Another huddle the following day after school, Silverwolf and Little Red at the center of it again—in over her head, whether she knew it or not.

William had taken his same perch as well, the cordless phone at the ready, but he had a tumbler of bourbon beside him now instead of a beer, and he'd brought the gun out this time, tucked it under his thigh.

Other things different too, like some of the rest of the world had sat up and taken notice. Even with some neighborhood boys in the huddle, others seemed to be watching from outside—maybe watching out for William himself, he recognized. Emma was sitting in her chair again, leaned forward, looked like her own phone in her hand. Some kids on the basketball court across the street kept missing shots, their attention divided. Another group sat on a stoop a couple of doors down, as if they were waiting—for what, William wasn't sure.

Silverwolf stepped out from the group, edged up toward William's house, closer than he'd ever come. Or—William remembered the sounds from the night before—closer than William had ever seen him.

"You spend all your time watching us out here, old man," Silverwolf said. "Maybe you should consider paying some attention to your own place."

"My place none of your business."

"Just looking out for the neighborhood."

"You ain't no neighbor."

Some laughter at that. One of the other boys gave out a "Thank God." Silverwolf moved a hand, just a flick of the wrist, for silence.

"Why don't you leave him alone?" came a voice from that stoop a couple of doors down. "Old man ain't bothering anybody."

"He bothered *me*," Silverwolf said. "The old man called the police on us"—pointing a thumb back toward Little Red.

The *us* rankled William as much as the *old man*. He felt the gun biting the underside of his leg.

"Just leave him be," the voice from the stoop said, and the body behind the voice rose up—a tall boy, broad shoulders, a leather jacket. William was suddenly reminded of worse times past.

Across the street, Emma stood at the top of the steps. Worried about him, William thought, and he was glad again her niece and nephew napped.

"Ain't no old man," William said—to both the boys, to all of them. "I can take care of myself."

More laughter from the huddle.

"Take care of yourself, sure," said Silverwolf. "That's all I'm saying, because we'd hate to have to take care of you ourselves."

"That a threat?" William asked, but the boy was already talking over him.

"Take care of your place too a little better. Looks like it could use a coat of paint, and you've got some loose boards there, a couple of loose nails. Somebody could get hurt."

William thought about the scrap of fabric from the night before, brushed his palm against the butt of his gun. "Seem like somebody already did get hurt. Found blood on my steps this morning."

Little Red tugged at Silverwolf's elbow, whispered something to him. He jerked himself away.

"Somebody else, I mean," the boy said.

Out of the corner of his eye, William saw the neighborhood boy on the stoop step forward, like he was going to walk into the middle of it all, but William just smiled. "Well, you right about that," he said, and casual-like, he lifted his hand and scratched the side of his temple with the gun, raising the barrel high to make sure everyone would see.

Some of the boys nudged one another, a few of them stepped away from the crowd—scattered. *Skedaddled*, William thought, not without pride. Across the street, Emma had ducked behind a post. The broad-shouldered neighborhood boy on the stoop had stopped, was shaking his head.

Little Red pulled again at Silverwolf's sleeve, but the boy stood firm.

"Listen up," said William. "No more walking down the middle of the road, and no more clustering up in front of my house. You leave all of us alone now, you hear? And especially that little girl there." He pointed vaguely toward her, the gun hanging loose in his hand. "She my daughter, I done shot you long before now."

As he spoke, William had believed that his words might change everything, releasing Little Red from the boy's hold, releasing the neighborhood itself even, returning the kids to the sidewalk, keeping them moving back and forth in a more orderly fashion, restoring the street traffic to its rightful flow.

His words did change things—and Little Red did release herself, releasing her hold on the boy's sleeve, stepping away from him—but none of it the way William had anticipated.

"*You* listen up, old man," she said. "I'm *nobody's* little girl."

Her voice surprised William, sounding older than he'd expected, brasher, spite behind it and a spitting too.

"He made you a woman, that it?" William said. "You his now?"

"I don't belong to anybody," she said. "I'm mine."

She pulled away from the boy, shot a hard look at William as she turned away.

"Watch where you point that thing," Silverwolf said, as he turned to follow her. "Awfully close to your own head there."

* * * *

A couple of hours later, William sat down for dinner: tomato soup and a grilled cheese sandwich, slices of tomato and bacon in the sandwich too. Comfort food, he thought, but try as he might, he could never get the sandwich to taste as good as when his wife had made it—or the soup either, for that matter, even though that was just pouring it from a can and heating it up with a little milk, same as she used to.

He thought about her as he ate. Seven years now since she'd passed, and not a day when he didn't miss her, her laugh, her presence, the way she looked at him. The way she looked at things generally, he thought, and he wondered what wisdom she might have offered about all this: the kids in the street, the phone calls, the noises in the night, the condom, and the confrontation this afternoon. The gun. The way it had all escalated.

"Kids," he could imagine her saying. "You called them kids, and that's all they are."

And what would he say to that? "High schoolers. Nearly adults. Adults soon enough."

"They're just walking down the street"—soothing, consoling—"they're not doing anyone any harm."

"Shooting daggers with his eyes, that one today."

"That's what teenage boys do. They posture. They puff themselves up. Don't take it too seriously."

"It *is* serious," he said. "Serious as a heart attack."

These last words he caught himself saying aloud, then regretted them. It had been a heart attack that had killed her.

Even if she'd been there, she'd have excused him for the slip. She had always been graceful like that, generous with another person's mistakes.

"It's the attitude," he would've told her then, same as he'd told Henry. "And then that girl, too."

"Times are changing," she would've reminded him.

"Old man—that what they keep calling me."

"Well, you *are* an old man." He could picture her smile as she said it. "But there's another way of looking at that phrase. This neighborhood, your neighborhood, you're the patriarch here. You've helped to build this place into what it is, you've invested in it."

She had always seen the bigger picture. Perspective, sounding board, conscience. His better half.

After he'd retired, it had been Sarah who'd encouraged the younger women in the neighborhood to ask his advice about how to care for their little gardens, encouraged William to help the children learn how to protect a root and touch a leaf, watched with pride as he reached down to cup his own hands around theirs, as he answered their questions about how to tend a plant that needed extra care. "Why are these leaves browning like that?" they'd ask, and "This yellow, this droopiness, is that too *much* water or not enough?"

"Too much, too little," he said to the image of his wife before him. "Everything need the right balance."

"And you've gotten out of balance," she said. "Your attention's elsewhere. Your *intentions* too. Your heart."

"Protecting the neighborhood," he told her.

She shook her head.

"Cultivating it is one thing. Defending what you've built is another. Looking for trouble ...."

"You been hanging too close to Henry."

He shook his head, trying to make sense of everything they were talking about—everything they *could've* talked about, he recognized, reminding himself again that he was alone.

"Do you really plan on using that?" Sarah would've asked at last. The gun sat beside his plate, not more than an arm's length from him now at any point of the day.

He wouldn't have known how to answer her. And pretty soon, the conversation in his head drifted off, the problem still unresolved, the image of Sarah fading before him as she waited for him to say something else.

He picked up the phone to reach out to Henry, then put it down. 12:00, 12:00, 12:00 blinked the clock. Whatever time it was, it seemed too late to call.

The sandwich in front of him was half-eaten. The soup had long since grown cold.

* * * *

When the noises started up again a little after midnight that night, William didn't wake in a panic, didn't call out his wife's name. He'd already been up, sipping his Wild Turkey, pondering on the world and his place in it.

Shadows rose and fell through the window blinds, pawing and gnawing at the back steps and at the walls of his house, and William imagined himself talking to Henry about it later, telling him it wasn't Little Red Riding Hood at all, but Hansel and Gretel for sure now, didn't matter whether they were related or who lived where or grew up where—a couple of bratty kids wandering where they shouldn't be, lurking around the house, nibbling away at the edges of it. Metaphorically speaking, he'd emphasize, talking Henry's talk.

But then he could hear what Henry would say. *And you're the witch then?* So maybe that wasn't the right way to explain it.

No matter what, they were at it again—their lovemaking too, if that's what you could call such a thing—while he sat inside like a prisoner, with his gun on his lap and the phone by his side.

Then that slow pulsing against the wall suddenly didn't sound like lovemaking at all, but more insistent, more sinister. The pulsing became a knocking, and then a slow pound, pound, pound.

This time he didn't hesitate to call, be damned if the police charged him or not.

A man answered. "9-1-1. What's your emergency?"

"They breaking into my house now."

"Who's breaking into your house, sir?"

"Hansel and Gretel," he said. "Little Red Riding Hood. That wolf, that same one."

"Wolves, sir?"

"That boy I done called about before."

"You've called before?" Fresh tension and a different confusion in the man's voice now. William heard the clacking of keys on a computer on the other end of the line. From outside, he heard a fresh round of scratching against the side of the house. He took a long swig of his bourbon, drained the glass without meaning to. Then on the line again: "Oh, yes, I see." No tension in the man's voice now, as if whatever he'd seen had explained it all away, and suddenly William saw a different story in the making.

"I ain't *crying* wolf, son," he said. "You send someone quick, okay?"

But there was no one on the other end of the line.

William pressed several buttons trying to get a dial tone again but heard nothing except the dull echo of an empty connection. He realized then what one of the new noises outside the house had been. The man on the other end of the phone hadn't hung up.

William dropped the dead line, let it dangle, gripped the gun more firmly.

He stepped back into the hallway. No more shadows climbing up the windows. But he thought he heard the front porch boards squeak. Hansel and Gretel up there now.

When the bell rang, he crept up to the door and looked through the peephole.

The girl was standing out front, her hoodie cinched tight around her face—Gretel back to Little Red, William figured, and ringing the door at grandma's house like always. She was alone on the porch, it seemed like, but then William saw Silverwolf's foot. Looked like his leg dangling across the arm of William's chair.

Little Red bringing the wolf with her this time, and then all the fairy tales blurring, because they'd underestimated him, if they thought he was just an old grandparently type, an old man. He could be the wolf himself, he could.

William watched her for a while, wondering what'd she'd say if he opened the door. It wasn't possible, he knew how the peephole worked, but he felt like she could see him too, and the moment he thought it, Little Red leaned back and stuck her tongue out at him—vulgar, her lips spread wide—then raised her face to the peephole, zooming into close-up, dark skin become a dark eye looming like she was peering back at him.

What big eyes you have. He couldn't help thinking that. *What big teeth.* But wasn't that reversing it all again?

His fingers tightened even more around the grip of the Colt.

The doorknob jiggled, but the deadbolt was locked. And then he heard her voice, "Anyone home?"—that same brashness and spite as the first time he'd heard her, but some laughter behind it this time, like this was all a joke and he was the butt of it.

The knob jiggled again and then shook, and then again, harsher, "Anybody in there?" and it came to him, what he should've told the man at 9-1-1, what he'd tell Henry later.

Not Hansel and Gretel, no, or Little Red either.

Goldilocks.

Didn't matter her hair wasn't blond, didn't matter her dark skin or how she'd grown up down the street, how she supposedly belonged.

Because wasn't something else at the heart of it? How some people crossed the line? How some people made a lot of assumptions about what was theirs, and then made themselves at home?

No Baby Bears maybe, no Mama Bear anymore. And William not a wolf or a witch but just an old grizzly, protecting what was left of his own.

A shadow at the window. William tried to make himself smaller against the door. "You in there, old man?" Silverwolf peering in, the boy, whatever he should be called.

Goldilocks rang the bell again—or whoever *she* was, Little Red, Gretel, Goldilocks, gook, what difference did it make? She rang it several times, then lay into it, the buzzer blaring, constant, echoing through the empty rooms. The doorknob shook again, and then the whole door, buzzer and door like an electric current running through William's body where he pressed against the wood, thinking of what he'd tell Henry. Tell whoever asked. An old story, one they'd understand.

Someone's been sleeping on my porch. (Wasn't that how it went?)

Someone's been sitting in my chair.

Someone's trying to come in and eat from my bowl.

In the distance, the sound of a siren. Close by, the ringing of the bell again, the jangle and shake.

William had waited long enough.

He unlocked the deadbolt.

He opened the door.

✗

Art Taylor is the author of *On the Road with Del & Louise*, winner of the Agatha Award for Best First Novel. His short fiction has won three additional Agatha Awards, an Anthony, a Macavity, and three consecutive Derringer Awards. He teaches at George Mason University. www.arttaylorwriter.com

EB AND FLO

Josh Pachter

"I ever tell you," my uncle asked, resettling his dark-blue McDonnell-Douglas baseball cap on his bald head, "how I met your aunt?"

"Why, no, Uncle Eb," I said. "I don't recollect having heard that story before."

This was a lie. I visit my aunt and uncle in their room at the Choctaw Nursing Home every Wednesday afternoon, and Uncle Eb tells me the story of the day he met Aunt Flo—who is my daddy's older sister—every time, usually more than once. This would be the second time today—but, hell, the man is 92, and tellin' me his three or four pet stories over and over again is just about the only entertainment he *gets* any more, if you don't count the old movies he watches on TCM.

"I's in the Army," he said. "This was durin' the war, 'round 1944, and I was in—oh, I can't remember the name of the place."

"Was that Santa Fe?" I prompted him.

"Santa Fe," he nodded, "'at's right. I was with a couple of my buddies, there was some kind of party goin' on out on the street, and this WAC was standin' behind us, watchin' the parade. She must of heard me talkin', 'cause she leaned over and tapped me on the shoulder and said,"—he scrunched up his face and squinted his eyes and squealed, in a voice that got a little more high-pitched and exaggerated by the week—"'Are y'all fum Miss'ssippi?'"

At that, Aunt Flo stirred. She is three years younger than Uncle Eb, but she's sunk pretty deep into the Alzheimer's by this point, and about all she does any more is sit beside him in her wheelchair and seem to be sleeping. For some reason the doctors can't explain, though, the woman can still spell. Her wrinkled eyelids flickered open, and she said, clear as a bell, "M-I-S-S-I-S-S-I-P-P-I, Miss'sippi."

"That's right, Aunt Flo," I said, and squeezed her hand, but her eyes were already closed again, and she was back in whatever country it was where she spent her days.

In 1943, Florence Farmer was a private in the Women's Army Corps and workin' at the Manhattan Project. Only 20 years old, she had been given a plum duty assignment as bookkeeper, which meant that, once a week, a motor pool driver and an MP took her into Santa Fe to pick up enough cash to hand Fermi, Teller, Oppenheimer, and the rest of the physicists and other laborers in the effort to create the world's first atomic bomb their weekly 30 pieces of silver. It was on one of those trips that she overheard PFC Ebenezer Schoolchild's Deep South drawl on a street corner and recognized a fellow citizen of the Magnolia State. They spent an hour together, explorin' the town, before she had to head on back to Los Alamos. They swapped addresses and began a correspondence that culminated, three years later, after Hitler's death in the bunker and Fat Man and Little Boy and the Japanese surrender, in a marriage that produced three children and had now lasted for more than six decades.

They had travelled the world together, Uncle Eb and Aunt Flo, but now their world had shrunk to this ten-foot by fourteen-foot room in West Hattiesburg, Mississippi, where their daughter Vi is the deputy district attorney for Lamar County. The staff at Choctaw treat them well, and they worship Willa, the South African woman who Vi, Marcus and Adam have hired to sit with them six days a week. Cousin Vi is there every evening at supper time, and I drop by on Wednesday afternoons.

This Wednesday, I was runnin' a little late, because I had spent the morning investigating the first case of murder Lamar County has seen since I was elected sheriff in 2012.

"You know what, Uncle Eb?" I said. "This week, *I* have got a story for *you*, if y'all are interested."

That threw him for a momentary loop. But he's a polite old feller, my elderly relative, and he blinked his eyes a time or two to reset himself into listening mode. "Go ahead then, son."

He knows I'm not his son. I'm never sure if he knows who I *am*, exactly—he calls me "son" because he can't seem to remember my name since we almost lost him to a stroke a while back. He always seems happy to see me, though, and I think he has the idea that I fit into the family somewhere.

"Well, sir," I said, "do you happen to recollect the Chevy dealership out on Weathersby Road, just west of the interstate?"

He nodded his head, and I have no doubt that he did. My uncle may be old, and he may repeat himself a mite and lose the thread of a conversation from time to time, but the man used to be a navigator on military aircraft and he still knows his geography.

"Owned by two brothers," I went on, "Jim and Carl Sullivan. Jim's full name is James Robert, but you call him Jim Bob at your peril— he's Big Jim at the Elks' Lodge and James to his wife Eleanor, and Jim to everybody else. And Carl, he's just plain old Carl, no matter who he's talkin' to. They got three or four salesmen out there at the dealership, a couple part-time mechanics, and Betty Anne Winston, who keeps the books."

Aunt Flo's eyes flickered open. "Mechanics," she said, as if she was taking her turn in an ordinary conversation. "M-E-C-H-A-N-I-C-S, mechanics."

"That's right, Auntie," I assured her, patting her hand. "Good job. Anyways, yesterday morning Betty Anne showed up at 8 a.m., reg'lar as clockwork, and opened the place up—and found Herbie Hutter, who is the senior salesman, been there 16 years, lyin' stretched out on the showroom floor in a puddle of blood."

Flo twitched at the sound of the word, but her eyes stayed closed and she didn't spell it. Uncle Eb was listening attentively, as focused as he is when Humphrey Bogart is a-putterin' up the Ulanga River with Katherine Hepburn on the TV.

"It wudn't until Betty Anne stopped screamin' that she realized Herbie wudn't dead, not quite, and dialed 9-1-1. As it happened, I was right nearby, so I wound up gettin' there a couple minutes before the ambulance. Herbie was still breathin', and I hunkered down beside him and asked him what had happened. 'Jim,' he said, that one word, clear as can be, and then he sort of sighed, and I knew he was gone. The EMTs tried to revive him, but it was no good. He was dead."

"Who was dead?" asked Uncle Eb, his brow furrowed beneath the bill of his ball cap.

"Herbie Hutter," I said. "Salesman out at the Chevy dealership on Weathersby Road? The one Jim Sullivan and his brother Carl own?"

"I think I remember Herbie. That man ain't got the sense God give a billy goat. When did he die?"

"He *died* yesterday morning, a little after eight. Coroner can't really tell when he was shot. Prob'ly sometime late Monday night."

"He got hisself shot?"

"That he did, Uncle."

"Who shot him?"

"Well, I heard him say 'Jim,' just before he died, and, sure enough, when I searched Jim Sullivan's office, I found a pistol in the top drawer of his desk. Gun's registered to Jim, got his fingerprints all over it, had recently been fired—and ballistics says the bullet that killed Herbie Hutter came from that very weapon."

To my surprise, Uncle Eb seemed to be following along. "Must of been him who done it, then, don't you think, son?"

"It surely does seem so. But Jim denies it. He swears he went to bed at 10:30, right after the news, and didn't get up till the alarm went off at 7 a.m. His wife Eleanor was in the bed with him, but she had a migraine and took a sumatriptan, slept about as sound as if she'd been under a general anesthetic. So Jim hadn't really got him a—"

"General," said Aunt Flo, rousing herself. "G-E-N-E-R-A-L, general."

"I met a general's wife once," Uncle Eb chimed in, like he'd been waitin' for a cue. "I ever tell you that?"

I sighed. "I don't believe you have," I said. "How did *that* happen?"

"It was after the war. I can't remember the general's name, but he was the Japanese guy in charge of that *thing*, that parade they had there."

"General Homma," I supplied. "The Bataan Death March."

"That's right, General Homma." As far as Uncle Eb was concerned, I had just taken a remarkably lucky guess. It never occurred to him that I had heard this story many times before. "Well, anyways, after the war MacArthur put him on trial there in—where was that?"

"The Philippines?"

"Right, the Philippines, and they flew his wife out there for the trial. And when it was over, we had to fly her back to Japan. I was the"—he growled in frustration at his inability to remember the details—"what do you call it?"

"You were the navigator on the flight," I reminded him.

"The navigator," he nodded. "We was headin' for Tokyo, and the wife come up to the cockpit and ast if we could fly over that mountain they have there—"

"Mount Fuji?"

"That's the one. It's a holy place for them or somethin', and she wanted to see it."

"So did y'all oblige her?"

"We surely did, and she was very grateful. She was a beautiful woman."

I nodded. "I love that story, Uncle Eb," I said. "Doesn't really he'p me with this case, but it's a great story."

He plucked a tissue from the box beside his chair and blew his nose thoroughly, then wadded it up and dropped it into the wastebasket.

"What case is that?" he said.

"Murder case. Seems like Jim Sullivan out at the Chevy dealership must of shot his salesman, Herbie Hutter, but he swears he didn't and—I don't know—I feel like he's tellin' me the truth. The gun *does* belong to Jim, though, and it's got his prints on it, and—"

My dear aunt opened her eyes and said, "Jim." But when she spelled it, the letters came out, "G-Y-M, gym."

I laughed. "Boy howdy, that's one way to spell it, Aunt Flo," I said, "but this time I mean the other—"

And then I froze.

And thought about it.

"Well, I'll be a dirty dog," I said. "I wonder …."

I leaned forward and kissed her wrinkled cheek, and it looked to me like the ghost of a smile danced across her face.

"I got to go check somethin' out, Uncle Eb," I said. "I'll come back and see y'all again directly, and this time I'ma bring y'all a little treat."

My squad car's Toughbook CF-30 connects to the internet, and *yelp.com* gave me eleven hits in and around the Greater Hattiesburg area: Gold's, World, LA Fitness, Curves, the Y, you name it. I started dialing my cell and struck pay dirt on the sixth call: once I managed to convince the woman who answered the phone that I was indeed a peace officer, she grudgingly agreed to check her records and, after I'd listened to an instrumental version of the Foundations' "Build Me Up, Buttercup" for what seemed like four hours on hold, came back on the line and acknowledged that, yes, Herbert Hutter was a member and, yes, he did pay $6 a month extra for the permanent use of a locker.

I burned rubber out of the Choctaw parking lot. If I had seen somebody else drivin' the speed I was drivin', I would of pulled them over and wrote them a ticket they would of had to take out a bank loan to pay.

The Hattiesburg Body Shoppe is on the second floor of an old brick building on Buschman Street, about halfway between Town Square Park and the Amtrak station, upstairs from what used to be the Ben Franklin five and dime when I was a kid and now styles itself an Italian *trattoria* but is in my humble opinion nothin' more than a common or garden-variety pizza joint.

I trudged up the stairs—I suppose an elevator would have defeated the purpose—and found Brandi, the bubbly youngster I'd spoken with on the phone. In all honesty, I would of rather had me *a* brandy along about this point in time, but that was goin' to have to wait. Brandi the Body Shoppe manager was a tall and slender thing in a skintight black leotard that left little to the imagination. Her long blond hair was tied back in a ponytail that juked and jittered as she led me down a corridor to the locker room behind the Nautilus machines and weight benches and recumbent bikes and treadmills and Stairmasters.

The lock on Herbie Hutter's locker was a combination padlock, and I fiddled with it for a minute before givin' up and goin' back out to my car for a crowbar.

"Hey, you cain't do that!" Brandi squeaked as she realized what I had in mind, lookin' at me like I had fell out of the stupid tree and hit every branch on the way down, but it only took me 30 seconds to show her she was wrong. And there in Herbie's locker, buried beneath a pile of dirty workout gear and a pair of black New Balance track shoes with the big orange N on the side, I found a nine by twelve manila clasp envelope that bulged enough to tell me it wudn't empty.

It wudn't empty. Inside it, I found an even dozen six by eight glossy photos that, given what they were photos *of*, I figure must of been printed off on a home printer and not run through the one-hour processing service at the CVS or Wal-Mart.

I recognized both the man and the woman in the shots, although I'm not sure I could put a name to some of the intricate positions they had managed to pretzel themselves into. The photographer had apparently been hiding outside the window, and he caught the copulating couple in what my cousin Vi would call *flagrante delicto* but the boys down at the station house would call *fragrant deliciousness* when there are ladies present and use a different F word to describe when they are amongst themselves.

I thanked Brandi for her help and apologized for the mess I had made of Herbie's locker. Ten minutes later, I pulled into Sullivan Brothers Chevy on Weathersby, parked my cruiser by the front door and found Carl in his office, holdin' down the fort in brother Jim's absence.

And when I handed him the manila envelope and he unfolded the little metal clasp and slid out the pictures, he cracked like an egg.

Carl was the naked man in the dingy motel room, and the naked woman was his sister-in-law Eleanor, Big Jim's wife. And when Carl finally stopped blubbering and I'd read him his rights, I was able to get the story out of him. No, he said, he didn't need a lawyer. He'd been terrified from the moment he pulled the trigger shortly after midnight on Tuesday, and he was ready to spill his guts.

He and Eleanor had been high-school sweethearts, but when Carl went off to Ole Miss, brother Jim—who had stayed home to run daddy's dealership—had cut in on him and swept her off her feet and married her. For the next 12 years, the young lovers had kept their distance out of respect for the sanctity of holy matrimony, but love or lust had finally overcome them, and eight months ago they had begun a torrid affair behind Jim's back.

Somehow, Herbie Hutter had tumbled to their goings-on, and one night he'd followed them to a no-tell motel 15 miles south in Purvis and photographed their frolics through the window they had carelessly omitted to curtain.

Y'all can see where this is going, right? Herbie had threatened to hand the pictures over to Jim unless Carl came up with $10,000 hush money. Carl didn't have a tenth that amount and couldn't see any way to get it. Desperate, he lied to Herbie, told him he had the cash and would meet him at midnight in the darkened dealership.

Carl kept the appointment—with the pistol he knew Jim kept in his top desk drawer in case of robbers in his gloved hands. He shot Herbie once in the belly, assumed one pistol plus one bullet equals one dead blackmailer, but panicked when he searched the body and discovered that Herbie—that lyin' bastard—didn't have the incriminating photos on him. So he stashed the gun back in Jim's desk where he'd found it and fled.

* * * *

First thing I did when I got to the station was order Big Jim's release, and then I had Carl booked and printed and stuck him in an interrogation room with a stenographer to take his statement.

I drove through Mickey D's on the way back to Choctaw, parked the black-and-white as close as I could get to the main entrance and carried my cardboard tray past the nurses' station down to room 128.

"Why, look who's here!" exclaimed Uncle Eb, as I came in the door. "I haven't seen you in quite some time, son."

It had been a little under three hours. I guess it's true what they say about gettin' old and startin' to lose your memory: you're always makin' new friends.

"I know," I said, "and I'm sorry. Things have been kind of crazy at work. But lookee here, I brought y'all some milkshakes. I got chocolate for you, Uncle Eb, and vanilla for Willa"—the cheerful South African giggled at the sound of that—"and Auntie Flo, I got you your favorite, strawberry."

Her eyes flickered open. "Strawberry," she said, pronouncing the word with great care. "S-T-R-A-W-B-E-R-R-Y, strawberry."

She took the cup in her liver-spotted hands and, eyes closed again, sucked pink goo noisily, happily, through the plastic straw.

⚔

Afterword

This story is a tribute to my Uncle Ben and Aunt Florence, who really did meet on a Santa Fe street corner in 1944, when he was a private in the US Army and she was a WAC attached to the Manhattan Project. For fiction's sake, I have changed my relatives' names and moved them south from the Northeast to Mississippi, but the story about General Homma's wife and Mount Fuji was a regular part of my uncle's repertoire and my aunt was a hell of a speller until the very end. They are both gone, now, and I miss them every day.

Josh Pachter's short fiction has been appearing in *EQMM*, *AHMM*, and elsewhere since the 1960s. In 2015, Wildside published *The Tree of Life*, a collection of his Mahboob Chaudri stories. He is the editor or co-editor of three collections that will be published in 2018: *Amsterdam Noir* (Akashic Books), *The Misadventures of Ellery Queen* (Perfect Crime Books), and *The Man Who Read Mr. Strang* (Crippen & Landru).

CRAZY CAT LADY

Barb Goffman

Someone had been in my house. I knew it the moment I pushed open the front door. The air felt heavy, tense, like a thunderstorm in the offing.

I scanned the room, glad for the bungalow's somewhat open floor-plan. The pillows on my comfy sofa remained fluffed. The yellow mums still stood tall in their vase on the kitchen table, their spicy fragrance filling the air. Everything was neat, as always. No drawers open. No mess on the floor. Things were exactly as I'd left them. Yet something wasn't right. Nothing made it clearer than Sammy's absence. My cat always greeted me when I returned home, butting his head against my legs. But Sammy was hiding, which made me wonder . . .

Was someone *still* in the house?

Call the police, a voice in my head whispered. *And tell them what?* another voice whispered back. *Everything looks fine. They'll think she's crazy.*

With a cold sweat breaking out on my forehead, I carefully set the grocery bags down by the front door. Some of Sammy's metal food cans clinked against each other. Church bells couldn't have sounded louder. I froze and listened hard. No reaction came from inside the house. The only sound I heard was the refrigerator humming. I took three small steps to the coat closet beside me and softly laid my head against its closed door. Was someone inside? I had to take several deep breaths to keep my heart from thumping like a drum so I could hear through the door. No one inside.

I hoped.

Steeling myself, I eased the sliding door open and leaned into the darkness. Boots, umbrella, jackets. And my trench coat. Long enough for someone to hide behind. With a shaking hand I reached forward and yanked it aside as I jumped back. But no one leaped out at me. No one charged at me with an ax. The closet, as they say on cop shows, was clear.

That left the rest of the house to check.

I clutched the umbrella by its long wooden handle and slowly, silently, crept forward. Even in an open floorplan, there were places someone could hide. Behind the couch? I inched toward it, raising the umbrella like a bat, approaching the arm, my heart beating rapidly, and … nothing.

What about behind the kitchen island? I crossed to the kitchen, biting my lower lip, twisting my head to see around the island corners. Nothing.

Rolling my eyes, I walked into my bedroom, grabbed the door, and poked my head around it. No one was hiding back there. Feeling a bit silly now, I headed to the bedroom closet. Nope. No one in there. No one under the bed. No one crouched behind the shower curtain. No one waiting to kill me in the spare bedroom or the linen closet or my office. Some papers beside my computer had been shifted, but that surely was Sammy's handiwork. The cat loved to walk on my desk, his tail swishing.

"Maybe I am crazy," I said.

Sammy peered at me from beneath the tan leather couch that sat angled to my desk, his pale green eyes narrowed. Odd. He usually lay on the couch.

"Maybe you should stop listening to those horror books in the car," he said. "They've got you spooked."

Okay, he didn't actually speak. But I knew what he was thinking, and he relied on me to voice his thoughts.

"I need to listen to those scary stories," I told him as I put the umbrella away, then carried the groceries into the kitchen. "They get me in the mood for my own writing."

I'd been working full-time as an author for nearly a decade now. I started out writing traditional mysteries, but over time I found my forte was suspense and horror. I became known as the woman who writes things other authors shied away from. Sadists who prey on the elderly. Predators who target babies. Sickos who hate dogs. And in this brand new book, I was focusing on a cat killer. Sometimes I couldn't believe the things I wrote. The few friends I had hated my books. So did a lot of people on social media, as well as the last guy I went out with. But my books sold. They sold big.

They're just fiction, I reminded myself whenever I began writing a distasteful scene. And I bought Sammy expensive food to ease my conscience.

I'd been writing one of those distasteful scenes earlier that morning—starting chapter one with a bang—before I took a break for errands. Now, I thought as I settled at my desk, it was time to dig back in. But … where was the file? I skimmed my computer's desktop. I always saved my current project there. No manuscript. Had I saved it in a folder by mistake? I opened the dog-book folder. Not there. I checked my ideas folder. Not there either. Not in temporary files. Not in my contracts folder. Not anywhere.

The file was gone.

A chill crept up my back, and I wheeled around, examining my office and the living room beyond. Had someone been in the house after all?

Don't be silly, Zephyr, a voice in my head said. *It's a technical glitch. The manuscript got erased somehow from the computer. Check the cloud. Your copy will be there.*

And it was. God bless modern technology. I saved a new copy to the desktop, made sure it was there, and began to type.

* * * *

Early the next afternoon, I returned home again and got a whiff of myself as I peeled off my windbreaker. Boy, was I ripe. At least today's sweat came from exercise, not fear. I ran seven miles every other day. My doctor encouraged me to pound the pavement since I spent so much time sitting and typing. But I'd run even if it weren't good for me because the activity often freed my muse, and I'd return home with good ideas for the next scene in my book. Today was no different.

In fact, I had such a great idea that I didn't even bother showering. I rushed to my computer, and—what the hell? The seat of my leather chair was all scratched up. Clawed in parts. Practically ruined.

"Sammy!" I yelled, turning around. He lay under the couch, staring at me, his pupils dilated. "What gives, Sammy? Since when do you wreck the furniture?" Other cats did, I knew, but Sammy had always limited his destruction to his many scratching posts.

I was so pissed off, I couldn't even bring myself to come up with a response from him. *Channel your anger into your writing*, a voice in my head said. So I did. Over the next three hours, a devastating scene poured out of me, as if I had experienced it and wasn't simply thinking it up as I wrote. It was a perfect follow-up to the torture scene I'd written first thing this morning—people eating live cats. And I'd been so engrossed, I barely noticed that my chair was now quite uncomfortable. I'd have to buy a new one.

I took a quick shower and headed out to my favorite office-supply store. One new leather swivel chair coming up. And while I was out, I bought two new scratching posts, too.

"Sammy," I called as I opened the front door an hour later. "Look what I have for you, baby."

Silence. Was this a new habit for him? No more rubbing against my legs when I returned home? The thought made me sad. He'd been my best friend since my mom died seven years ago. In fact, Sammy had been Mom's idea. Right before the cancer killed her, she urged me to buy a baseball bat for protection—my books had taken a darker turn and I'd started getting death threats—and a cat for company. That's how Sammy became part of the family. It was a relief to have him to talk to. I'd never been good with people, but Sammy and I hit it off the second we met at the shelter. Until now. What was going on with him?

I set one of the new scratching posts in the living room, the other in my office. I spotted Sammy peering at me from under the couch again.

"Well, I'm home," I said. "Not that you care anymore."

"Since when do you guilt trip me?" Sammy asked.

"Since when don't you love on me when I come in the door?" I said.

No response.

Hmph. I shoved the clawed chair into a corner, then headed outside to get the new one from the back of my SUV. As I stepped off the porch, I stumbled. Not like me at all. I looked back and noticed a corner of the welcome mat (with the perfect saying on it: Go Away) was tucked under itself, leaving the surface uneven, which must be why I nearly fell. At least there was an explanation for *something* today. I quickly smoothed the mat out, grabbed the chair, and carried it over the threshold.

"This is not for you," I told Sammy as I wheeled the new chair to my desk. "If you must ruin furniture, use the old chair. Now, who's ready for dinner?"

That lured him out. He followed me into the kitchen, and I dished out his favorite meal, Chicken of the Sea solid-white albacore. I wasn't above bribery to make him love me again, and I could swear I heard him purring while I whipped up a veggie stir fry. After dinner we both returned to my office. I always did my second author job—social media—in the evening, after I met my daily writing quota.

I settled into my comfy new chair, and Sammy stretched out on his usual spot on the couch, where he could keep an eye on me and most of the house. It seemed the tuna bribe had worked. Yay. It would be the perfect thing to tell my fans about on Facebook, except I never shared such personal details. I'd have to come up with something else.

I skimmed Twitter for five minutes and Facebook for ten—my limit—looking in vain for inspiration for a post. Ultimately I typed off a quick "Thrilled that so many of you are enjoying my newest book, *Tortured Innocence.*" And I included my name as a hashtag. Then I switched over to email. My inbox was filled with the usual amount of fan mail, hate mail (obvious from the creative subject lines, such as "Die, Bitch, Die"), and normal, never-ending spam—except for one email that caught my attention. Its subject line read, "Nice orange tabby."

My mouth hung open. Very few people knew I had a cat. I never mentioned him publicly. Never shared pictures of him. I kept my private life private. With a growing sense of unease, I clicked the email open.

"Just because it's fiction doesn't make it okay. People who write about cat torture should face the same agony. Your time will come, hypocrite."

Hypocrite?

The last guy I went out with—a disastrous blind date last week—had called me a hypocrite when I said I liked cats. Dan knew I was an author before we met, and I think he went on the date just to give me crap about my books. When I mentioned my next book would involve cats, he got vicious. Life was too short to deal with horrible people, I'd thought, so I thanked him for a *lovely* meal, set money for my unfinished dinner on the table, and left the restaurant.

I thought that would be the last I'd hear from him, but apparently not.

I clicked *reply*, ready to fire off a response. Then a voice in my head weighed in: *Don't engage. That's what he wants. Don't encourage him.*

You're right, I thought. I moved to delete the blank email when I noticed the name in the *to* line. It was my name. What the hell? The only way my name could show up in the *to* line when I hit reply was if I was the original sender.

With goosebumps marching up my arms, I clicked back to the original message to inspect the sender information, and there was my name and email address. Son of a ... So Dan apparently was some kind of computer whiz and had gotten creative to freak me out. What an asshole. He—

I stopped short as I focused on the subject line once more. *Nice orange tabby.* I'd never told him that. Never even said I had a cat, just that I liked them. The only way Dan could know about Sammy—and that he was an orange tabby—is if he'd been in the house.

My thoughts drifted back to the prior day, how I thought someone had broken in, then decided I was scaring myself for no reason, my imagination spurred on by the horror book I'd been listening to in the car. But I didn't imagine Sammy not greeting me at the door yesterday, as he usually does. He was hiding when I came home. And he was agitated today, destroying the chair. So maybe Dan really had been in the house.

"Is that what scared you yesterday, Sammy?" I whispered, swiveling around, looking for signs of Dan. "Is that what got you so upset today? Did Dan sit in my chair?"

And, I realized, two more important questions loomed large. Had Dan been in the house again today? And was he still here?

I grabbed a large dictionary off a shelf—not much of a weapon, but at least it was hard and heavy—and tiptoed to the storage closet in my office. You'd probably have to be pretty small to hide in there, but better safe than sorry. With the dictionary lifted, ready to throw, I yanked the closet door open. And exhaled. No one was in there. Whew. Just reams of paper, boxes of toner, other office supplies on the top shelf, and what I'd come for, my baseball bat.

I curled my fingers around it and, with Sammy at my side, searched every inch of the house. No signs of Dan. No signs of forced entry. All the windows and doors were secure. Unless he were a magician, Dan couldn't have—

My eyes flew wide as I remembered tripping off the front porch that afternoon because the edge of the welcome mat had been curled under. I hadn't even paused to wonder how the mat had gotten bent like that. But now that I thought about it, that couldn't have happened naturally. Maybe I shifted it somehow when I was leaving and didn't notice, but it seemed more likely that someone must have moved the mat. I didn't keep my spare key under it, but if someone were searching for a key, that would be a likely place to check.

I flipped on the outside light, and with a flashlight in one hand and my bat in the other, I stepped onto my front porch. I had a swing out there with a couple of pillows on it. The swing was creaking back and forth in the cool autumn breeze, as if someone had just eased off it. I looked around. Couldn't see anyone. Couldn't sense anyone. I returned my gaze to the swing. I kept a spare key inside one of the pillows. Slowly I unzipped it and felt inside. The key was there.

But had it been taken out, used, and then returned? I couldn't tell. Swallowing hard, I grabbed it, then turned around and stared out into the darkness. Raising the bat high, I hoped I appeared fearsome to anyone who might be out there. *I won't let you scare me, you jerk.*

Then I stormed inside with the key, slammed the door, locked it, and pushed a table against it. Tomorrow I'd change the locks.

* * * *

I awoke the next morning bleary. I'd barely slept after having a terrible argument with my friend—ex-friend now—Jeanine. Dan was her cousin. He'd moved to town a few weeks ago, and Jeanine had begun badgering me immediately to go out with him. Eventually I agreed, though romance wasn't high on my agenda. After the disastrous dinner, she'd prodded me for details, and I'd merely said he wasn't my type. No use hurting her feelings. But after I realized last night that Dan had broken in, I called and gave her a piece of my mind. Why had she set me up with someone who clearly wasn't right in the head? Someone who was a huge jerk and now, apparently, a stalker? She actually defended him, saying that while she could imagine him losing his temper—he loved animals—he'd never break into my home. Never.

"And maybe you wouldn't have this problem if you didn't write such appalling things," she snapped.

That had been the final straw. I cursed at her and hung up. Our friendship was over. For the next ten minutes, I stomped around the house, alternating between muttering and yelling, slamming doors, and punching the couch cushions. I grabbed the baseball bat and nearly swung it, aching to destroy a framed photo of Jeanine and me that sat on the bookcase beside my office closet. But I stopped myself, dropping the bat. Sure it would feel good to shatter some glass, but I might miss some shards when I cleaned up and Sammy could get hurt. I couldn't risk that.

Now in the morning light, I was certain I'd made the right decision to end my friendship with Jeanine. But it still upset me terribly, and after a night of tossing and turning, I had a cobwebby brain to boot. Not good for writing. But I was a professional, and a professional writes, so I slurped down two cups of coffee and forced myself to focus. I wrote a vicious scene in which fur flew—literally. I'd nearly finished it when the locksmith arrived. While he did his thing, I texted Maggie, the only real friend I had left, and asked her to meet me for lunch. I needed to talk about what had happened with Jeanine. A half hour later, with a new key in hand for the front and back doors, I was off.

"Don't worry, Sammy," I called just before heading out. "You're safe now."

* * * *

I met Maggie at her favorite restaurant. The booths were soft and private, the wait staff was always attentive without being overbearing, and their head chef had his own Michelin star. I never cared much about food, but at least what they served here was tasty and healthy. Yet today I couldn't enjoy it. I nervously rubbed the white tablecloth with my thumb while I waited for Maggie to select her meal. I'd quickly chosen smoked hummus with walnut-crusted seitan, but Maggie always liked to try something new. And she seemed to be taking longer than usual to decide, focusing intently on the menu. Finally after I'd downed my second glass of Diet Coke, she chose the lasagna cruda, we ordered, and I leaned forward to unburden myself.

I filled her in on everything that had happened recently, including the date with Dan, my fight with Jeanine, and how I'd feared someone had broken in two nights ago, but had come to think I'd scared myself over nothing.

"Turns out, it wasn't nothing," I said.

Wrinkling her nose, Maggie shrugged.

"What does that mean?" I might have said it a little loudly. A man at a nearby table glanced my way.

Maggie sighed, straining the buttons on her blouse. "I'm sorry, but maybe you're being a little dramatic. Yeah, you had a bad date, but you don't have any evidence someone broke into your house."

My eyes bulged. "Hello? What about the welcome mat? And the deleted computer file? And the email about my orange tabby?"

Our meals arrived, and after taking a bite, Maggie starting ticking off on her fingers. "You might have moved the welcome mat yourself when you stepped on it. You said that yourself. Your file could have gotten erased through a computer glitch. You *thought* that yourself. And the cat reference—someone could have spotted Sammy through the window. He does sit on the sill sometimes."

"Maybe. But how do you explain the use of the word hypocrite in the email?"

Maggie flapped her hand, as if my concern was ridiculous. "That's a normal word. Anyone could have used it. Anyone who knows you're writing a book about a guy who tortures cats and then sees a cat in your window could think it."

I swallowed some hummus, trying to not be defensive.

"Well, who knows the topic of my new book? I can count on one hand the number of people I've told. You, Jeanine, my agent, and my editor. And I told Dan, stupidly. Only you, Jeanine, and Dan live here. Did you tell anyone?"

"No. Believe me, it's not something I want to talk about."

"What does *that* mean?" I'd never noticed this tone from her before.

She set her fork down, her mouth drawn in a thin line. "I'm sorry, Zephyr, but you don't make it easy to be your friend sometimes. Writing the things you do. When you first started writing horror, I thought it was a random book and you'd return to writing plain old mysteries with non-gory murders. But no. You actually enjoy the sick stories you write." She wiped her mouth with her cloth napkin. "You want the truth? When I read your new book about the guy who rapes babies a few weeks ago, I nearly threw up. And yet I've hung on. Been your friend. You can't imagine the number of times over the years Jeanine and I have defended you, and now you've blamed her for trying to help. Cursed at her?"

My mouth hung open. I hadn't mentioned the cursing. So she'd spoken to Jeanine already.

"You think Jeanine tried to help me? You think setting me up with a guy who broke into my house, terrorized Sammy, and tried to scare me to death is helping? Are you kidding?"

"Jeanine tried to help you by setting you up with a nice man who might distract you from the terrible thoughts that run through your brain," Maggie said. "We thought that maybe if you had some goodness in your life, it would be reflected in your books. And once again, you don't know Dan did those things."

"Really? Then how do you explain the email coming from *me*?"

"Maybe you were spoofed. Or maybe someone finally got so fed up with your revolting books and decided to try something—anything—to get you to stop." She stared at me so hard I thought her eyes might pop out of her head, and it all became clear.

"You? You did it?" Maggie's son was good with computers. I bet he could have taught her how to spoof me. "You scared me to death."

"Me?" Her face flushed. "I didn't do anything. Now you're getting paranoid."

"Am I?" Tears flooded my eyes. "I thought you were my friend. I can't believe this." I sprang from the booth and tossed money on the table. "Don't worry about having to defend me anymore. We're through."

She stood and laid her hand on my arm. "I hate to say it, Zephyr, but maybe it's for the best. You're not the person you used to be. I hope you can find a way out of the darkness in your life."

The tears I'd been fighting escaped my eyes, and I stormed off, sped home, and went straight to my computer. I signed onto Facebook and unfriended and blocked Maggie and Jeanine. Then I unfollowed them both on Twitter, erased their numbers from my phone, and sank onto my office couch, sobbing. I hadn't cried that hard since Mom died. I'd been friends with Jeanine and Maggie for years. What was I going to do now? Without the two of them, I had no close friends, no one to do things with, no one to confide in. I only had three old friends from college whom I spoke to maybe twice a year, and a few acquaintances I knew from my Horror Writers of America meetings, which I attended sporadically at best. I wasn't friendly with the neighbors. I had no family nearby. I was alone.

Except for Sammy, I realized. I still had Sammy.

Wait a minute. I swiped the tears off my cheeks. Where was he? I'd been so upset when I came home, I hadn't noticed his absence. Sammy might have been spooked by what had happened over the last couple of days, but he always comforted me when I was upset, crawling into my lap, snuggling close. Until now.

"Sammy," I called, my voice echoing through the house. "Sammy!"

No response. I headed out to the main room, checking his favorite spots. He wasn't lying in the ray of sunshine on the shag area rug, right below the back window. He wasn't perched on the front windowsill, watching the birds that liked to taunt him. He wasn't even sitting in the cardboard box he'd commandeered last week after I'd emptied it out.

This wasn't normal. "Sammy, you're scaring me," I called. "Where are you? This isn't funny."

But still he didn't respond. And I began to wonder if maybe Maggie hadn't spoofed me. Maybe Dan was behind all these tricks after all. Had he broken in again? Is that why Sammy was hiding now?

Stop scaring yourself, a voice in my head urged. *Sammy's under the couch in your office again. It's just a new favorite spot for him.*

That had to be right, I thought, nodding repeatedly as I hurried back into my office and peered under the couch. But Sammy wasn't there.

"Sammy, come out," I yelled as I stood up. "Please! Stop scaring Mama."

I strained my ears, listening for his paws on the floor, padding along, coming to calm me down. But I waited in vain.

Call the police, a voice in my head whispered. *And tell them what?* another voice whispered back. *That her cat is hiding in the house? She can't tell them there's been a break-in. Everything looks fine. They'll think she's crazy.*

I broke into a sweat, realizing that once more I needed to search the house. I tiptoed to the office closet to grab my baseball bat. I reached my hand out and … wait. The door wasn't fully shut. Hadn't I closed it yesterday? I blinked, trying to think back, but I couldn't remember, too distracted by the whoosh of blood roaring through my ears.

Focus, Zephyr. Swallowing hard, I inched toward the door, craning my neck forward like a turtle emerging from its shell, and tried to listen as hard as I could. I heard nothing. Just my own heavy breathing. Surely Dan wasn't hiding in the closet. He couldn't be. I reached forward, grasped the knob, and pulled the door open.

"Mrrow!" Sammy yowled.

I screamed as he jumped from the closet's top shelf, his claws slashing my neck and cheek before he bounded off. I stumbled backward, tripped over the bat—which I apparently hadn't put away last night—and lost my footing. I windmilled my arms but couldn't keep from falling. It all seemed to happen so slowly. "Sammy," I yelled as I banged my temple against the sharp edge of the desk, then collapsed onto the floor, my head slamming hard against the wood. I slapped my hands against my stinging skin. Blood coated my right palm at my temple and my left-hand fingers at my throat.

Too much blood. I'm losing too much blood, I thought, after lying lightheaded for a few moments. I tried to rise, but the room spun and vomit rose in my throat. I threw up, then clunked my head back against the floor.

As I lay there, growing more and more woozy, I realized that if I died, Sammy would be in trouble. He had no food in his bowl. He'd run out of water in a day or two. And since I cut ties with Maggie and

Jeanine, no one would come to check on me, so no one would come to check on Sammy.

I tried to crawl toward my phone but didn't make it more than a few inches before I drained my energy. Besides, I realized, the phone was on the desk. How would I reach it?

"Meow," Sammy said from behind me. He swished past my feet, then jumped up onto the desk, beside my computer. If only I could get him to push the phone to me. But that wouldn't work. Cats were smart, but they didn't do things like that.

"I'm sorry, Sammy," I said, my voice weak. "I'm so sorry."

He stepped onto the keyboard. A pop-up screen appeared, asking, "Are you sure you want to delete this file?" My eyes widened as I watched Sammy delete the cat book. Then he somehow opened a new file in Microsoft Word and began stepping on the keyboard again.

"I tried to get you to stop."

I watched Sammy's words appear on the screen. I must be hallucinating, I thought. Sammy couldn't type. He was a cat for God's sake.

Right?

"Maybe Dan did break into the house, and everything I'm doing now is a hallucination," Sammy typed. "Or maybe you're finally seeing things clearly."

My head swam. Had Sammy deleted the original file? Shredded my chair so I wouldn't write? Sent the hypocrite email, which is why it came from my account? Had he purposely jumped at me from the closet, scaring me, slashing me, hoping something like this would happen? No. That was insane. It was the type of thing I'd write, not the type of thing that actually happened.

Yet here we were.

"But if I die, Sammy, then you'll die, too. No one will be coming for us."

"Think of all the cats that will be saved when your book isn't published," Sammy said. He jumped down from the desk and nuzzled against me. "All the evil people who won't get bad ideas from you. It will be worth it."

"Besides," he said, biting my cheek, "I'll have food for quite a while."

⚹

Barb Goffman has won the Agatha, Macavity, and Silver Falchion awards for her short stories, and she's been a finalist for national crime-writing awards nineteen times, including for the Anthony and Derringer awards. Her book, *Don't Get Mad, Get Even*, won the Silver Falchion for the best short-story collection of 2013. Learn more at www.barbgoffman.com.

A PIE TO DIE FOR
Meg Opperman

"Palisades apartments. Thirty minutes," a familiar voice said on the other end of the line. "I'm extremely eager."

My breath caught. My insides tingled. I could feel heat stealing its way up my neck toward my cheeks. It had been a couple months since I'd last heard Benedict's voice. We'd taken a bit of a break—I was a newlywed, after all—but now it seemed we were back on.

"Yes, thank you. Goodbye," I said in a neutral tone so my husband wouldn't become suspicious.

Hanging up the phone, I walked over to the half-made pumpkin pie—my third attempt—and knocked the pumpkin puree off the counter.

"Oops! I can't believe I did that!" A puddle of puree spread across the kitchen floor. "Now I have to go to the store again."

My husband Tom chuckled, turning from where he was washing dishes. "Annie, calm down. It's just my mother, for Pete's sake, not the governor."

I blew a strand of hair off my damp forehead. "Easy for you to say. *You* aren't the one in charge of the perfect Thanksgiving dinner." Our first Thanksgiving as a married couple.

"I'll think it's perfect because you made it. If my mom doesn't like it, so what? She'll get over it." Tom wiped his hands on a towel, came over, and wrapped his arms around me. He leaned in, lips grazing my forehead. "Maybe we can't have pumpkin pie, but how about a little dessert?"

"Tom!" I swatted his chest, stepped out of his embrace. "Be serious. Your mom *loves* pumpkin pie. It's the highlight of the meal for her."

"Fine, fine, let a man starve at his own feast." He grabbed a sponge and knelt to clean up the pumpkin mess.

Glancing at the kitchen clock, I snatched up my purse and keys, headed for the door. "Thanks, hon. I'll be back soon. We need anything else?"

"No, and you don't need to go. I bought extra cans of pumpkin at Harris Teeter last night. Just in case. Look on the bottom shelf in the pantry."

No, no, no! I could feel the minutes ticking away while I was stuck making a stupid pie for Tom's ungrateful mother.

"Thomas Alan Oakley! You sneak!" I said, in mock outrage, "What if I'd succumbed to your charms and given up on that pie? I'd be in the doghouse with your mother, all so you could get a little action." And I'd miss getting some on-the-side action of my own.

"Can't blame a guy for trying." He looked up from the floor, a lopsided grin on his face.

"Oh yes, I can." I glared, but my giggles ruined the effect. Okay, what other ingredient could I run out of?

After I grabbed a new can from the pantry, Tom said, "Babe, would you mind turning on the radio?" Now back at the sink, he held up his soapy hands. "Can you believe the governor's in town today? Giving a speech in front of the new food pantry. The hypocrite! I can't wait to vote him out of office!"

My sweet, do-gooder husband had been unsuccessfully lobbying the soon-to-be-former-governor to quash a bill that would lower the maximum household income for receiving food stamps. A lost cause, but Tom took his *pro bono* work seriously.

Switching on the radio, I went back to my pie.

Tom continued to grumble. "The man cuts money to education. Maybe he can give a speech in front of a school next? And how about a small business while he's at it?"

I nodded sympathetically. "Politics is messy."

I usually liked talk radio, but why would anyone care to listen to that blowhard? Well, except my mother-in-law. She was a big supporter, despite Tom's protests. She'd actually applauded when the governor loosened gun control laws. Loosen gun control? As far as I was concerned, only experts should handle guns. The rest were just statistics waiting to happen. But I wasn't going to change Tom's mother's views any more than she'd change mine.

Setting myself back to pie making, I could only find an 8 ounce can of sweetened condensed milk. The recipe called for 14 ounces. How *fortuitous*.

"Looks like I'm headed to the store anyway," I moaned. Did my voice sound guilty? Maybe I should call Benedict back and cancel? I *was* a married woman now and shouldn't go sneaking off whenever he called.

Tom didn't seem to hear me, his attention glued to the radio.

I picked up my purse and keys and hurried toward the door.

"Where're you going?" Tom called.

"Store," I called back. "Not enough sweetened condensed milk."

"I saw a can of it in the spice drawer."

Damn! I came back and checked the spice drawer. One can of sweetened condensed milk.

"I wonder what it's doing here? I must have been so nervous with your mom coming …"

He grunted, his attention on the radio.

Returning to my pie, I glopped condensed milk into the mixture. Why was I going through all the trouble? I didn't even *like* pumpkin pie, and Tom's mother was sure to criticize my efforts … even though I'd made the crust from scratch.

"Annabelle, have you ever considered working outside the home?" she'd asked on more than one occasion. As though all I did was sit around eating bonbons. If she only knew how hard I worked. I took a moment to enjoy my stunning kitchen, just the right blend of colors and patterns to make it pop. I have a good eye and a steady hand. Not that she ever noticed.

Whoops! I'd stirred too hard, slopping pumpkiny goo over the countertop. I'd clean it later—I had to hurry. I reached for the egg carton, but it was empty. "You didn't use all the eggs, did you?" I asked. Did my voice sound too hopeful?

Tom opened the fridge, handed me a fresh carton. Giving me a wink, he went back to scouring pots. Yes, I'd burned a few of the side dishes. In the end, everything turned out fine … except the pie. Third time's the charm, right?

I cracked in the eggs, fishing out a large piece of shell. Why was cooking such a big deal, anyway? I was good at lots of things. Just not cooking. I added the cinnamon, a little salt, a hint of ginger. But no nutmeg. Tom's mother adored nutmeg. Said it made the pie. I rummaged through the spice drawer, making as much noise as possible.

"What's wrong?" Tom called over his shoulder.

"No nutmeg."

"She probably won't even notice—"

"Seriously, Tom, who are we talking about here? She was a food critic! She'll notice." Once again I snatched up my purse and keys.

"Didn't we have some in the—"

"Be back soon! Love you, bye!" I slammed the door behind me and clambered into my Volvo. I slipped on a pair of red driving gloves—the best present my mother-in-law ever gave me. Throwing the car in reverse, I screeched out the drive.

Passing the Harris Teeter a couple of blocks from home, I sped up. I still had time, but it'd have to be a quickie. Just something to relax me before a day spent with my mother-in-law. Was that so selfish?

Fortunately, traffic was light. I sped past a Food Lion and a Giant, then hopped on the highway for a couple miles. Exiting, I coasted into the Palisades apartment parking lot, a four-story complex across from the new food pantry. The apartments were still under construction, but the gate had been left open. Four lanes separated me from the food pantry lot, but even from here, I could see a crowd of people and reporters clustered around a podium, listening to the great blowhard himself. At least the weather was nice. A sunny, windless November day.

I pulled around back and parked. Climbing out of the car, I quickly opened the trunk and wheeled out a floral print overnight bag—a girl should always be prepared. I headed to the backdoor and examined the lock. A piece of duct tape had been put over the clasp, preventing it from latching. Perfect.

I hefted my bag and took the stairs straight to the fourth floor. There I found the door leading to the roof. More tape. Excellent.

Once on the roof, I searched for the best spot, unzipped the overnight bag, tipped my equipment out, and examined each piece. Assembling it, I placed the scope last. I checked my throwaway phone. Less than a minute. Not bad.

Normally, I'd opt for my bolt-action M-24. But Benedict had specified "extremely eager"—code for "terminate with extreme prejudice." I shoved the .408 high-explosive round clip into the HTI. I *aimed* to please.

I checked and rechecked the wind speed. Still calm. Lock and load, baby. I slid the barrel out a few more inches, making sure nothing blocked my shot, and set the tripod into position. Not an easy target, the distance my greatest concern.

I waited until I had my shot, took it. The top half of our esteemed governor turned to something closely resembling my pumpkin pie filling. *Eww*. Hate to be in the front row. Guess Tom's mother would have to find another candidate to support. Like I said, politics is messy.

But no time to enjoy the show. Breaking down my rifle, I stuffed it into my suitcase, and as I exited the building made sure to snag the tape off the doors. Hitting the road as fast as possible without drawing attention to myself, I merged into traffic and jumped back on the highway.

On the way home, I swerved into the Food Lion parking lot, near the dumpsters. I made a quick phone call.

"You heard?... Um hmm. Nice doing business with you again ... No, Benedict, the pleasure was all mine." I disconnected, pulled the battery and SIM card from the phone, and reached into my glove box for a small hammer I kept there for just such an occasion. I used it to break the phone and SIM card, then rolled down the window and tossed the pieces into the dumpster. Sighing, I added my red gloves to the pile…gunpowder residue. Couldn't be helped. I'd pick up another pair at Macy's, and my mother-in-law would never be the wiser.

Continuing on, I stopped at Harris Teeter and bought nutmeg. When I reached home and parked in the garage, I left my floral case in the trunk. There'd be time enough to clean everything later, when Tom wasn't home.

Walking into the kitchen, I found Tom staring at the radio like it contained the secret of life.

He rushed over and hugged me tight.

"Hey, hey, I just went to the store," I said.

"Did you have your radio on? You hear the news?" He let me go.

"What news?" I took a step back.

"Someone assassinated the governor!"

"No! That's crazy," I said. "Why would someone do that?"

He shook his head.

"Well, at least I managed to get the nutmeg for your mom's pie." I held up the bottle.

"Huh? Oh, yeah, I sent you a text. Found the nutmeg in the back of the spice drawer. It must have been hiding." He pointed to a bottle of it sitting next to my half-made pie.

"Oh, I can't believe I didn't see it! Well, there can never be too much spice in life." I measured out the nutmeg, stirred it into the mixture, then poured the pie into the crust. "I hope your mom enjoys it. She has no idea the trouble I went through to make this pie."

✗

Meg Opperman, a cultural anthropologist by training, has had short stories published in *EQMM*, *SHMM*, *Weird Tales*, and various mystery anthologies. She writes a column (Write Side Up) for the *Washington Independent Review of Books* and won the 2015 Short Story Derringer for her story, "Twilight Ladies."

MURDER AT MADAME TUSSAUD'S

Dan Andriacco

Albert Poe, one of the senior employees of the world's most famous wax museum, took a personal pride in introducing new attractions. This showed in his voice even as he addressed the last tour group of the day.

"Now, ladies and gentlemen, Madame Tussaud & Sons is proud to present the latest terrifying addition to the Chamber of Horrors: Ormond Struthers, the infamous 'Grosvenor Square Ghoul' who chopped the heads off his victims and lined them up on a shelf in his flat."

The display caught the madman at work, a fiendish grin on his face. He had just used an axe to secure the latest addition to his collection of severed heads, which belonged an unfortunate fellow named Peter West. The waxwork head, with yellow hair and staring blue eyes, lay on the floor.

"Cor, don't it look real!" A man who bore a strong resemblance to a hedgehog looked, not at the head, but at the body of the victim.

Poe chuckled. "Yes, a bit too real for some, I shouldn't wonder. Don't get too close, ladies!"

"Even the blood looks authentic, the way it's dripping from the poor man's neck," said a stout, matronly woman. Ignoring Poe's instruction, she stepped forward. "Why, it's—"

The woman dropped her purse and screamed. She was still screaming five minutes later when John Theodore Tussaud himself, Madame's great-grandson and manager of the museum, arrived at the Chamber of Horrors and directed Poe to summon Scotland Yard.

* * * *

Or so Poe reported. I wasn't there. I learned about the murder at Madame Tussaud's a few hours later from an enterprising young constable, Fishpaw by name, who stopped by my flat on his way to the crime scene. He shared the bare details: decapitation in the wax museum's Chamber of Horrors.

"This is better than I expected." I handed over the agreed-upon gratuity for alerting me to any sensational murders that came his way. It was 1888, the Year of the Ripper, and all London was on edge, but I never expected a slaying so promising as this. I was in such a good mood that I threw in an extra half-crown.

"Oh, and who's in charge of the case?" I asked Fishpaw as he turned to leave.

"Inspector Richard Catchpool, sir."

Within minutes I was out of my dressing gown and into my coat and a cab. After a brief stop at the telegraph office, I arrived at the Alhambra Theatre in Leicester Square. I raced into the big old pile, barely noticing the fanciful poster of Professor Carlo Stuarti levitating a fetching young lady in a nightgown, and barged into that worthy's dressing room without knocking.

Still clad in white tie from the evening's performance, Stuarti cut a dashing figure—in his early sixties, over six feet tall, pure white hair except for one dramatic black streak matching the color of his mustache, and as strong and fit as me at twice my age. He regarded me with amusement as I paused in the doorway to catch my breath.

"What is it, Jack?" he asked. "Murder?" His melodious voice, honed from years on the stage, hinted only slightly to his Roman birth. He spoke French, German, Spanish, and a few other languages just as perfectly as he did English, according to those who would know.

"Yeah, but not in Whitechapel, Boss. Much, much better."

"Well, then. The curtain rises." Looking not at all displeased, he picked up his silver-headed walking stick and his top hat. "*Andiamo!*"

The great man said little in the cab. As close as we were, the man billed as "the Count of Conjuring" remains as mysterious as one of his magic tricks. Was Carlo Stuarti really the natural great-grandson of Charles Stuart—Bonnie Prince Charlie—as he claimed? I don't even know whether he believed it himself. I only know that he was greatest magician I ever saw.

* * * *

Madam Tussaud's had moved to Marylebone Road the previous year, before I came to England to promote Buffalo Bill's Wild West Show. The place was crawling with coppers, there to keep nosey-parkers like Stuarti and me away from the museum and the macabre murder within. We quickly found a walrus-mustached sergeant who looked authoritative. I ignored Constable Fishpaw, who stood at his elbow pretending he didn't know me.

"Inspector Catchpool sent for us," I lied.

The sergeant looked from me to Stuarti, decided it wasn't his business to wonder why the Inspector wanted an American and a toff, and let us through.

"The Chamber of Horrors is this way, Jack," Stuarti said once we entered the building. "I have spent many enjoyable hours there."

This did not surprise me.

The *Madame Tussaud & Sons' Catalogue* from 1888, which sold for sixpence, sits on my desk to refresh my memory of that grotesque night. But I don't need it. The creepy waxwork models stick in my mind as though they were the genuine article. William Marwood, Her Majesty's hangman, with sad eyes and thinning hair over a high dome. Charles Peace, the notorious Banner-Cross assassin and Blackheath burglar, stared at the floor; his beard scraggly and his forehead wrinkled. Burke and Hare, who killed at least sixteen of their fellow Scots and sold the bodies to medical students, faced each other like mirror images. Those portraits were among the top attractions of the Chamber of Horrors, though there were dozens of others.

Some nameless bard many years before had written:

> *I dreamt that I slept at Madame Tussaud's*
> *With cut-throats and kings by my side,*
> *And that all the wax figures in those weird abodes*
> *At midnight became vivified.*

But it wasn't quite midnight yet. And it's the flesh-and-blood body—especially the blood part—that sometimes returns in my nightmares, though later I saw worse in the Great War. We turned a corner after seeing an exhibit devoted to Guiteau, the assassin of President Garfield, and came upon the corpse unexpectedly. Several coppers of various ranks hovered about a portly man in a grey pinstriped suit. He pondered the bleeding, headless cadaver as if he had nothing better to do and looked up with a frown. "What are you two doing here?" he demanded. "How did you get past my men?"

"Inspector Catchpool?" I ignored these perfectly reasonable questions. "My name is Jack Barker and this is Professor Carlo Stuarti, better known to enchanted audiences the world over, including crowned heads of Europe, as the Count of Conjuring." The boss paid me a lot of money to boom him, and I was always on the job.

As I paused dramatically, Catchpool regarded Stuarti with naked skepticism. "Oh, a Count, are you?"

"Actually, my good sir, I'm—"

"Here to help you," I said hastily. This was no time for Stuarti to announce that he was, by rights, King Charles IV, sovereign of the United Kingdom of Great Britain and Ireland, with Emperor of India thrown in as a side job. The "Count of Conjuring" moniker was my alliterative brainstorm, and I'm still proud of it. (In an unaccountable fit of modesty, he had rejected "The Lord of Legerdemain.") "Professor," on the other hand, was a common honorific for prestidigitators in those days.

"Let me explain, Inspector," I added.

Stuarti could saw a woman in half with the best of them, even Devant and Maskelyne, but mind-reading was his signature stunt. Having dabbled in the art myself, the first time I saw him I realized he was a master of what's known in the trade as "cold reading." He spotted small clues and could make accurate inferences about people. They would swear he had to be reading their minds. After a few weeks as Stuarti's press agent, I hatched the idea of using his talent to solve a sensational crime that had baffled Scotland Yard. Stuarti saw the genius of it immediately. His name would be splashed across the front page of every newspaper in London, and maybe beyond. All we needed was to get in early on the right case—and here we were. But of course that's not what I told Catchpool.

"Professor Stuarti has an amazing talent at what has been called the science of deduction," I said. "He's generously volunteering his valuable time to help you discover who perpetrated the horror in the Chamber of Horrors." I liked the way that last rolled right off my tongue.

Catchpool's chuckle in response took me completely off guard. "Oh, that won't be necessary, Barker," he said smugly.

"And why not?" Stuarti demanded.

"Because we know who the killer is. The Grosvenor Square Ghoul is up to his old tricks again."

"But he's in Newgate Prison, awaiting his date with the hangman," Stuarti objected.

"Not any more, he isn't. He's been on the loose since this morning."

So the Ghoul had escaped and claimed another victim, leaving the headless body at the exhibition devoted to him in the Chamber of Horrors? This was the crime story of the century! I had to get Stuarti involved before the press arrived.

"Who was victim?" I asked.

"We don't know just yet," Catchpool said, with a light air that suggested this was but a trivial detail. "There was no head, save the waxwork one, and no identification. The corpse was wearing the clothing of the wax figure he replaced."

"Then there are still mysteries to be solved," Stuarti commented cheerfully. "Who is the dead man and what happened to his clothes? Surely he didn't arrive naked!"

"Inspector Catchpool?"

We all turned toward the speaker, a handsome young woman with a perfectly proportioned figure gift-wrapped in a paisley print dress. Soft blond curls peeked from her bonnet above large violet eyes. She wore a silver crucifix around her lovely neck.

"Who are *you*, then?" The tone of the Inspector's *basso* voice wavered between exasperation and outrage.

"Aurora O'Reilly, *The Daily Telegraph*. I'm here to report about the murder. Your sergeant was kind enough to let me in."

Catchpool's eyebrows shot up almost to his thinning hairline, boding ill for the kind sergeant. "A woman?"

"Your powers of observation are not to be denied, Inspector," Stuarti said drily. He knelt by the body.

"Murder *is* a little out of mine," Miss O'Reilly confessed. "I usually cover fashion, society, and gardening. But I was the only journalist in the office when a wire came through saying that a headless body was discovered in the Chamber of Horrors. That seemed like a front-page story to me, especially with all that fuss in Whitechapel. Who knows when one of my male colleagues would show up?"

Catchpool looked murderous. He turned to his men. "All right, who called in the Press? Out with it!"

No one answered. Not even me. I tried to look innocent, but what would be the point of Stuarti helping Scotland Yard solve a sensational murder without a journalist on the scene to record it? That would be like a tree falling in the forest with no one to hear it. I intended to get headlines for the boss. Hence my stop at the telegraph office before rushing to the Alhambra.

Stuarti looked up from the body and finally broke the silence.

"The unidentified victim was something less than middle age and comfortably middle class. These are not the hands of a working man." He stood, apparently finished with his pronouncements, and studied the floor.

"This is the Count of Conjuring, the famous Professor Carlo Stuarti," I told Miss O'Reilly as he worked. I spelled the last name. "He is a consultant to Scotland Yard."

"He is not—"

"Did you notice these footmarks in the dust, Inspector?" Stuarti said, interrupting Catchpool's eruption.

"What footmarks?"

"I'll take that as a 'no.' Look here." He pointed. "Those marks from a pair of square-toed boots lead to that storage closet and back again." He tried the closet door. "Locked."

Violet eyes wide, Miss O'Reilly scribbled in a notebook.

"Hopkins!" Catchpool bellowed.

"Yes, sir!" A fresh-faced young constable came forward, fairly clicking his heels in his eagerness.

"Tell Mr. Tussaud we need to get into this closet."

"Yes, sir!"

Hopkins left, post-haste.

Stuarti looked at me with an enigmatic smile. He had tools in his pocket, used in his act, that would have opened the lock in about ten seconds flat. But the Inspector wouldn't be an appreciative audience.

"What do you think is in the closet, Professor?" Miss O'Reilly asked.

"The victim's clothes, most likely. I've been wondering where they are."

John Theodore Tussaud, sculptor and chief artist of the eponymous museum as well as its manager, showed up within a couple of minutes, key in hand. About thirty, with a thick waxed mustache, he moved like a man shouldering a heavy burden. Gossip maintained that the museum was underfunded, despite its fame and popularity.

"This is terrible," he muttered as he stuck the key in the door. "Nothing like this has ever happened since my great-grandmother opened the museum more than half a century ago."

"Don't worry too much," I said. "Miss O'Reilly's headlines won't hurt business. In fact, brace for a big crowd tomorrow."

Tussaud didn't respond, but I could see wheels turning in his head; they were the wheels of commerce. He opened the closet door. Catchpool, gently shoving him aside, squeezed into the closet and pulled out three things: the headless wax figure of the Ghoul's final victim, a tweed suit, and a bowler hat.

"I recognize that apparel," Tussaud cried. "It belongs to William Cobb, one of my best wax artists. What a loss! I saw him just this morning, putting the final touches on our likeness of the Grosvenor Square Ghoul."

"Maybe the Ghoul didn't like his work," I suggested, earning a gratifying smile from Miss O'Reilly.

Catchpool, less pleased with my witticism, gave me a dirty look before he asked Tussaud, "Do you think you could you identify Mr. Cobb's body minus his noggin?"

"You mean …" Tussaud, turning from the clothes, studied the corpse. "Well, the size is about right. It could be he."

"Was Cobb a married man?" Stuarti asked.

He paused. "Yes. Why do you ask?"

"The dead man is wearing a wedding ring. Why did you hesitate before answering, Mr. Tussaud? My question was simple enough."

"It's a little embarrassing, that's all. I dislike telling tales out of school, but Cobb didn't act as a married man should. Let's just say he liked the ladies and they liked him back. His missus has arrived a few times looking for him. She thought he would be here and he wasn't. That put me in a very awkward position, as you might imagine. I equivocated, to avoid getting the scoundrel in domestic trouble, but she knew what he was up to."

"Why do you think the Ghoul hid the clothes?" Miss O'Reilly asked Catchpool, delicately changing the subject.

"He wasn't hiding them—he just tossed them out of the way," Catchpool said dismissively.

"Then why did he lock the door?" Stuarti objected. "And where did he get the key?"

"From his victim, no doubt. He found it when he went through Cobb's pockets looking for money to aid his escape. And as for why, you might as well ask why he collects heads. Ormond Struthers is a madman, a lunatic. You can't expect his actions to make sense, Stuarti."

"No, of course not," Stuarti said.

But I could tell the magician had something up his sleeve.

* * * *

Stuarti always arrived at the Alhambra hours before his performance. I found him there late the next morning, lounging in his dressing gown of royal purple.

"How was your dinner with Miss O'Reilly?" he asked.

I cocked an eyebrow in inquiry.

"You're wearing the same jacket you wore last evening, Jack. The amount of that Simpson's-in-the-Strand bill sticking out of your pocket indicates that you didn't dine alone, and you haven't mentioned any young ladies of late." The boss was a one-woman man and she was deceased, but he took an endless interest in my social life. "A late supper with Miss O'Reilly was a simple deduction. She is a good Catholic girl, I trust."

"I'm afraid so," I said gloomily. It didn't take a Count of Conjuring to catch the meaning of her crucifix. "I slaved away for you the whole evening anyway. She wanted to hear about my work with Buffalo Bill and Annie Oakley, but I kept bringing the topic back to your brilliance with the murder. It paid off."

I plunked a copy of *The Daily Telegraph* on his dressing table. The headline across the top of the page screamed "HORROR IN THE CHAMBER OF HORRORS." I claim no credit for that; great minds think alike, that's all. Below was the subhead, "Famed Magician Helps Identify Victim." The accompanying illustration showed said victim, William Cobb, who sported a small beard beneath his mustache.

"I saw that," Stuarti said. "Good work, Jack."

But I snatched the paper back and read the story to him anyway, imaging the sensational events told in the dulcet tones of their author:

By A. O'Reilly
Special Correspondent

Ormond Struthers, the notorious "Grosvenor Square Ghoul," escaped from Newgate Prison on Wednesday and immediately launched a new reign of terror by beheading a wax artist at the Madame Tussaud & Sons' wax museum in Marylebone Road.

The body of William Cobb, 32, was discovered in the Chamber of Horrors during a late afternoon tour. It had been substituted for a wax figure of the Grosvenor Square Ghoul's most recent previous victim, Peter West. Cobb's head was missing, presumably the first of a projected new collection by the ghoulish killer.

Struthers had been awaiting execution for committing at least seven murders by decapitation in the Grosvenor Square area over two years. Scotland Yard later found the heads of all the victims on a shelf in his flat in Mayfair. He had been a private tutor of banjo lessons.

"This heinous crime shall be the Ghoul's last," affirmed Inspector Richard Catchpool of Scotland Yard, in charge of the case. "We shall capture Ormond Struthers and bring him to justice once again."

"I guess they'll have to hang him eight times now," I said. "But I don't actually remember the Inspector uttering that quote to Miss O'Reilly."

"I'm sure he would have if he'd thought of it," Stuarti said with a wry smile.

I continued reading aloud:

Professor Carlo Stuarti, an illusionist and psychic currently performing at the Alhambra Theatre and famed throughout Europe as "the Count of Conjuring," helped identify Cobb by leading police to a storage closet where his clothes had been secreted away by the murderous madman. Mr. John Theodore Tussaud, manager of the family-owned museum, identified the body as that of the artist who, ironically, had formed the wax figure of the Grosvenor Square Ghoul.

The story went on to say that the Ghoul had been spotted in Whitechapel, the West End, Norwood, and basically all over Hell's half-acre.

"Where do you suppose he really is?" I mused.

"I don't know, but I'm sure he was never in Marylebone Road yesterday."

"What!"

"Struthers didn't kill Cobb, Jack. I didn't believe that for a minute. It's just too convenient. The Ghoul's escape from prison on the same day as the opening of the exhibition devoted to him in the Chamber of Horrors gave somebody a perfect opportunity to get away with murder. But I'm going to make sure that doesn't happen."

I whistled appreciatively. "That's an even better headline, Boss." I was thinking something like: "MAGICIAN SOLVES MURDER IN WAX." "What's your first move?"

"I've already made it. I visited the Widow Cobb this morning."

"Catchpool won't like that. Didn't he say before he kicked us out last night to keep your Roman nose out of this?"

"He won't know my nose was in it." Stuarti pointed toward a dark beard and wig on the dressing table. "I visited her in the guise of Mr. Stuart King, of the Adelphi Assurance Company. 'I've come about Mr.

Cobb,' I said. 'Are you one of the husbands, then?' she asked. 'Are you one of the men Bill cuckolded?' It wasn't a pleasant conversation, I assure you, but I had to meet her."

"What for?"

"To see how big she is. It was just barely possible that a woman of Amazonian proportions might have slain Cobb with an axe, particularly if she drugged him first. But his wife is barely five feet tall and slender. She also looked worn out, possibly from taking care of the four lads hanging on her apron. She appears a bit older than her husband, perhaps forty."

"You've ruled her out as a jealous wife, then, even though she knew about Cobb's dalliances?"

"Ruled her out as a jealous wife who turned to murder, you mean? Yes, I've eliminated her from suspicion. A woman motivated solely by love turned into hatred would almost certainly act alone, and not ask her brother or father for help. Mrs. Cobb simply wasn't physically capable of committing this murder by herself. But there was another possibility. Do you see it?"

I pulled out my briar pipe, wishing I could light it. Stuarti had a crazy idea that tobacco is unhealthful. He also refuses to eat meat. It took me a minute of unaided concentration, but I finally replied. "Maybe she wasn't jealous, but just the opposite. Maybe Cobb wasn't the only one stepping out. If she had a lover, he could have swung the axe for both of them."

"Exactly. However, I am certain from spending a lifetime on the stage—and even more certain from observing the emotional ways of performers when they are off the stage—that the dried tears on Mrs. Cobb's cheeks were genuine. She also asked me very few questions about the possibility of a settlement from a life insurance policy that she was unaware of. Surely a murderer would be more interested in the prospect of financial reward, even if that were not the primary motivation. Mrs. Cobb's dress is at least five years out of date and the children's clothes are well patched."

"Still, whether she was interested in that mythical money or not, it wasn't kind of you to raise her financial hopes."

Stuarti looked hurt. "You should know me better than that, Jack. Mrs. Cobb's plight has moved me. I will make sure she does not go wanting, though she need not know the identity of her benefactor."

"Well, you haven't come up with much for a morning's work, Boss."

"On the contrary! The morning was well spent. I have all but elim-inated the person who would undoubtedly be Inspector Catchpool's prime suspect if it were not for the convenient availability of the Gros-venor Square Ghoul. Of course, that leaves an unknown number of jealous husbands who did not appreciate Mr. Cobb's attentions to their spouses."

"What are the chances we'll ever learn their names?"

"I already have them." As if by magic, Stuarti produced a small pocket diary. "Clearly the women listed here are not Mrs. Cobb's dressmakers and hair dressers. My hand was quicker than her eye when the good lady was kind enough to show me her late husband's rather untidy study."

"Ha! You're almost as good as I say you are."

The conjuror bowed theatrically. "I'm tempted to give this to Catchpool, though. Interviewing all these women is just the sort of thing Scotland Yard excels at, I'm sure."

"How would you explain to the Inspector your ill-gotten posses-sion of the diary?"

"I would send it to him anonymously."

I shook my head. "No glory in that, Boss."

"Nevertheless, there might be justice. And I'm more interested in the mystery of the missing head. That's more my line than the dull routine of interviewing obvious suspects."

"What mystery? What do you mean?"

"Why cut off the victim's head, Jack?"

"To make the murder look like the work of the Grosvenor Square Ghoul. That's obvious."

"Yes, but why do that? Why go to all that trouble, which even involved the cumbersome task of dressing the victim in the clothes of the wax figure and then hiding the figure? That's not obvious. And what happened to William Cobb's head? It wasn't in the closet with the clothes and the figure. That would have been an easy place to stash it and eliminate the possibility that the killer would be caught with it. The Ghoul collected all the heads he severed, but it's not likely his imitator has adopted the same peculiar habit."

"Unless he's just as mad."

Stuarti waved that thought away with a typically Italian gesture. "I do not accept the possibility. There is method in this murder, not madness."

"So we're back to motive. If the killer isn't insane, then he must have had a reason to kill Cobb." After a moment I snapped my fingers, energized by creative inspiration. "John Theodore Tussaud! There are all kinds of motives for him to murder his employee—a woman, or a rift between artists, or even a publicity stunt to boost ticket sales. And nobody had a better opportunity to put the body in the Chamber of Horrors than the manager of the museum."

Stuarti looked thoughtful. "You know, Jack, that's not complete-ly—"

"Professor Stuarti?"

We turned with a start to the doorway of the dressing room and the woman standing there. She was attractive, though not handsome in the way of Miss O'Reilly, pleasingly plump, and well dressed. I put her age in the mid-twenties. She clutched a parasol as though it were a life-preserver.

"My name is Clementine McNutt. I'm here because I read about you in the newspaper today. You're a very clever man and Scotland Yard won't take me seriously. I need your help. Of course, you know nothing about me—"

"Only that you are a milliner and greatly concerned about your fiancé, whose initials are H.G."

She had a wonderfully expressive moon-shaped face, and now it expressed astonishment. "How in the world did you know all that?"

"He's the Count of Conjuring, that's how," I said.

"Tiny bits of felt and glue that attached themselves to your dress make your employment obvious enough," Stuarti explained. "But if you weren't very upset, you would have cleaned them off before you left your shop. You didn't even don a hat, which is highly unusual for any young woman. and all the more so for a milliner." Magicians aren't supposed to reveal how they accomplish their effects, but some-times Stuarti couldn't help himself.

"I have a little shop on Saxe Coburg Square, true enough. And how did you know about my fiancé?"

"That charming locket around your neck is inscribed 'To C.M. from H.G.' Obviously, you are the 'C.M.' Inasmuch as you are wear-ing an engagement ring, it would be peculiar indeed if the locket and ring didn't come from the same source. Ergo, Mr. H.G. is your fiancé. However, he didn't accompany you. The inference is that he is in some way the reason for your visit, and also the source of your distress."

"You are quite right on every point, Professor. I can see that I have come to the right place since the police have been of no help."

"Let us hope so. Tell me about your fiancé, then."

She paused, gathering her thoughts. "His name is Henry Goode, with an *e*, and he is good indeed, a wonderful man. We met at a church picnic over the summer. He works as a minor clerk in a government office in Whitehall, but with strong prospects for advancement as he is intelligent and hard-working. We became engaged only a fortnight ago, the happiest day of my life so far. He was to meet me at my parents' home last evening in Kensington for a small celebration in honor of the occasion. He never arrived, gentlemen. My father, who dislikes Henry, seized upon this mysterious behavior as a sign of moral weakness. But I am quite convinced there is some darker explanation."

"Maybe there was an emergency at Whitehall, a secret affair of state that he couldn't talk about even to you," I suggested. My mind naturally runs in such directions.

"But Henry told me he was taking a holiday yesterday. He'd been working so hard of late—something to do with the Portuguese in Africa. And when I visited his landlady, she told me that he went out yesterday morning and didn't come back."

"Your concern is understandable," Stuarti said. "How long ago was that picnic where you first met Mr. Goode?"

"A little more than four months."

"That is a quick engagement, though I have known quicker."

"It didn't take me long to know my heart, nor he his."

"But surely, Miss McNutt, his life has not become a completely open book to you in so short a time. Perhaps an old bad habit he has managed to conceal has landed him into some trouble, such as a penchant for gambling, or opium—"

"Or women! You might as well say it."

The possibility that Henry Goode had scampered off with a woman not his fiancée had certainly been on my mind, perhaps influenced by all those female names Stuarti said were in the late William Cobb's pocket diary.

"And if that is the case," Stuarti said, "you would be better off without such a man."

Sometimes he lacks tact.

Storm clouds gathered on Miss McNutt's round face. "That's exactly what my father and that horrible man at Scotland Yard said!" she cried. "But my Henry and I had no secrets from each other. I know he is a good man and he's missing. Yet the police won't even try to find him until more time has passed. I expected better from you, sir!"

"Please calm yourself, Miss McNutt. I didn't say I wouldn't try to help. I'm willing to look into Mr. Goode's disappearance, but only if you are sure you want to know the truth."

She had the good sense to think about that before responding. Then a look of resolve settled on her features. "I do want to know the truth, Professor. Whatever it is, it will affect the rest of my life."

* * * *

Some hours later, Stuarti and I stood on the front steps of a building in Montague Street, just around the corner from the British Museum.

"I'm a Scot myself," he told the formidable woman blocking the door.

"You dinna look it and you dinna sound it."

"My family had to leave Scotland rather suddenly some time ago."

Clearly, the great man's smooth patter worked no magic on Mrs. MacLeod, Henry Goode's landlady. Unimpressed by his evening clothes and fancy walking stick, she wasn't letting us into her tenant's flat.

The Count of Conjuring had turned in his usual flawless performance that evening, ironically including an illusion called "the headless princess." He assured me later he hadn't given the two investigations that had fallen his way the slightest consideration while on stage. "The best way to solve a problem is to forget about it for a while," he said.

But Mrs. MacLeod was turning out to be a problem that couldn't be forgotten.

Stuarti put on a dejected face. "I don't know how I will explain this to Miss McNutt. She'll be so disappointed."

"Mr. Goode's young lass, you mean?"

"Yes. She's very concerned about his disappearance."

"I ken that."

"She asked me to find him as a favor to her. I'm hoping that perhaps he left behind some clue in his rooms."

"Weeeell, now, if it's for the lass..."

Stuarti saw a crack in her armor and squeezed through it. "You needn't worry that we'll take anything. You can stay in the room and watch carefully as we search. I'm sure you're a very busy woman, but I'm happy to reimburse you for the time that would involve."

This was a meaningless bit of stagecraft, of course, given that Stuarti could make an elephant disappear in front of an audience of several hundred carefully watching people.

I don't know whether Mrs. MacLeod's eyes popped because of the pound notes that appeared in Stuarti's hands as he made the offer or because there were so many of them, but within seconds the cash disappeared into her ample bosom.

"Come to that, I'm sure Mr. Goode wouldn't mind you having a look around if it puts Miss McNutt at ease. This way, gentlemen."

Goode lived in sparse bachelor quarters not unlike my own, with a few comfortable chairs and cluttered tables. Stuarti's piercing eyes swept the room. Within a few moments he picked up a folded copy of *The Morning Post*. "Look at this advert, Jack."

MADAME TUSSAUD'S EXHIBITION
(Baker-Street Station)
THE CHAMBER OF HORRORS

THE GROSVENOR SQUARE GHOUL

Ormond Struthers
See the Madman at his Work!
Every Relic connected with the Case
ADMISSION, 1s; CHILDREN, 6d
Open from 9 a.m. till 10 p.m.

"The Chamber of Horrors again!" I said. "That's some coincidence."

"It's no coincidence, Jack. Henry Goode spent his last day on Earth at Madame Tussaud's. We must go there right now!"

"But the museum will be closed at this hour."

Stuarti shot me a pitying look. "Surely you know no lock can defeat Carlo Stuarti!"

* * * *

"I still have no idea what this is all about," I said. My voice echoed in the creepy darkness of the wax museum after hours. My Smith & Wesson, which Stuarti insisted I bring, felt good in my hand, even though I was no Annie Oakley.

"We are up against a very clever foe," Stuarti said, shining his pocket lantern before us. "Scotland Yard was fooled by his misdirection, the basis of all magic tricks. But I, a master of illusion, saw through it to the real question: Why was the victim's head missing? Yes, the police were supposed to think that the Grosvenor Square Ghoul, newly escaped from prison, was starting a new head collection. That was surely the point of staging the gruesome tableau. But why was it necessary they think that? *Misdirection!* It kept Scotland Yard from wondering why the victim's body was headless. And the reason it was headless was *so that it wouldn't be identified.*"

"But Tussaud *did* identify the body."

"No, Jack, he misidentified it, as he was expected to. Cobb's clothes were planted in that closet, where the police were sure to find them eventually, to lead to that conclusion. The body is that of Mr. Henry Goode."

"Why was he killed, then?"

"To provide the body. That was the primary reason, and perhaps the only one. Now the killer must destroy the head to permanently prevent identification. There's a perfect means to do that in a wax museum, a means not available last night, with Scotland Yard on the scene until the museum reopened this morning. The killer never left this building. He's been hiding until he could dump Goode's head into a vat of boiling wax."

* * * *

I felt a growing desperation as we searched room after room. And in the end, we were almost too late. I could scarcely believe that William Cobb, looking haggard and unkempt but still recognizable from his image in the *Telegraph*, stood at a burbling vat with a grisly object in his hand. It was like a scene out of Hell, with a room temperature to match.

"Stop!" Stuarti called to him. And then, to me: "Jack, your gun."

I pointed the Smith & Wesson at Cobb, hoping my hands didn't shake. I'd only ever fired the weapon once, and that was at a rabbit nibbling my mother's lettuce back in St. Louis. I'd missed.

"The museum is closed," Cobb said coolly. "Who are you?"

"I hope that Mr. Tussaud and Scotland Yard will overlook my ill-manners this once," Stuarti said. "Who we are isn't important, but we know who you are and what you've done."

"Why did you kill Henry Goode?" I blurted.

"Was that his name?" Cobb looked at the head in his hand, bizarrely reminding me of Hamlet and Yorick. "The poor fellow had the misfortune to be just my size, or close enough. And that meant that he would fit in the wax model's clothes and later be mistaken for me. We didn't have the dimensions for the Grosvenor Square Ghoul's seventh victim, so I modeled his figure on my own. That's what gave me the idea that Bill Cobb should die—that and the Ghoul's timely escape from prison to take the blame. A body in my clothes without a head might be suspect, but not with the Ghoul on the loose. And death seemed the perfect way out for me. If I only disappeared, you see, my creditors and certain young ladies might keep looking. It all came to me in a flash, and when I saw a man about my size I knew it was his fate to be my salvation. I even put my wedding ring on the corpse to seal the identification. I won't be needing it."

I finally understood. "You had some kind of woman trouble and you took the unmanly way out."

"Unmanly!" Cobb cried. He stood on the raw edge of madness—whether that was the result of cutting off a man's head or the cause of it even Stuarti could never know. I tightened my grip on the revolver, praying that the wax artist cared enough for his own life not to force me to shoot. "A lack of virility is not my problem, Yank," he went on with a sudden bark of laughter. "Rather, I am plagued by an ungodly fertility! The ladies in question are becoming quite insistent that I live up to my responsibilities."

Then several things happened all at once. Cobb threw the head at me and ran toward the door. I fired my revolver and kept firing until it ran out of bullets. Stuarti, who was closer to the door than I, pulled a sword from his walking stick and walked rapidly toward Cobb. Just then the door opened and a sleepy-looking guard demanded, "What's going on here?"

Cobb crumpled about two feet from the door, his left leg a bloody mess.

"I hit him!" I cried in amazement.

* * * *

"How awful for you!" Miss O'Reilly exclaimed over dinner at Goldini's Restaurant in Gloucester Road the following evening. By that time John Theodore Tussaud was already sculpting a model of "the Waxwork Killer" for his next big exhibit.

"Well, it was no day at Coney Island," I said modestly.

"How in the world did you manage to shoot him in the leg?"

"By aiming for his mid-section."

The lady journalist had already reported the story for the *Telegraph*

("KILLER CAUGHT AT MADAME TUSSAUD'S") with reasonable accuracy. Detours from the truth weren't her fault. I embellished on unimportant matters to boom Stuarti, so the subhead became "Throws Severed Head at Famed Conjuror." A few details remained to be cleared up. That was as good an excuse as any for dinner with the comely miss.

"How did that dreadful man manage to hide in the museum for a whole day without getting caught?" Miss O'Reilly asked. "I thought the Yard searched the building thoroughly."

"Remember, Cobb worked for Tussaud's for years and even though they were in a new building, he knew every nook and cranny. He changed his hiding places as Catchpool's men moved along in their search. That's what Stuarti thinks. He also speculates that Cobb had help from a friendly female employee who alerted him to the progress of the coppers. She most likely would have been his next victim."

"My word! Professor Stuarti is amazing, isn't he?"

"Oh, he's a marvel, all right. But even Homer nods now and again. The boss is upset with himself because he should have observed that Cobb's wedding ring was loose on Henry Goode, who didn't bear any sign of having lost weight." I put my fork down, shocked by what I just admitted, undercutting the great man's air of infallibility. "You mustn't print that! Promise me you won't print that or I won't let you in on his next case."

Miss O'Reilly's violet eyes shone.

"His next case? You mean you think he'll solve more spectacular crimes?"

"You can bet on it."

Dan Andriacco is the author of twelve mystery novels, including the Sebastian Mc-Cabe - Jeff Cody series. His most recent books are *Queen City Corpse* (September 2017) and *House of the Doomed* (2018), a Sherlock Holmes pastiche. A member of several Baker Street Irregulars scion societies, he frequently speaks at Sherlockian conferences and meetings.

ROOSTER CREEK
John M. Floyd

Katie Harrison swallowed hard, took a deep breath, and looked out at the greenish-brown plains and hills stretching away to the horizon. Sparrows flitted and chirped in the branches overhead, and even in the dappled shade the midday sun was warm on her shoulders. But Katie barely heard the birds, barely felt the heat.

Underneath her feet, the chair shifted an inch, and her heart lurched. She winced as the noose tightened around her neck. The fingernails of her bound hands bit into her palms, behind her back. Then the wobbly chair on which she stood stabilized and she let herself breathe again. Above her, although she couldn't see it, the rope was looped over the limb of an oak that had once supported a wooden swing that she'd played on as a child, twenty years ago.

Ten feet away and to her left, a silent and stone-faced woman with red hair sat and watched from a second chair. Beside the redheaded woman stood a huge black man in a battered hat and bib overalls. His face, usually relaxed and peaceful, had a pained look. Katie had met both of them only a month earlier, after she'd trudged empty-handed and muddy all the way up the wagon-rutted road from the town of Perdition. Only a month. In one sense, the time had passed quickly; in another, it seemed like years since she stepped down off the stagecoach from Lincoln Wells and asked the old fellow behind the counter in the stage office where she could hire a buggy to take her up the old north road.

Ain't much out that way, he had said to her, hunched over his paperwork.

I know, she'd replied. *That's where I grew up.*

* * * *

The old man behind the counter looked up at her over the top of his glasses, then leaned back, squinted out the window at an open shed behind the office, and shook his head. "Sorry, young lady. We do rent buggies here, but they're all being used."

Just as well, Katie thought. Her funds were limited anyway, and she recalled she had once walked the three miles home from Perdition when she was a kid. She could do it again.

With fond memories in her head and a cheap travel bag in her hand, Katie Harrison set out on foot beneath an overcast sky, heading for what she thought would be a quick and pleasant visit, for one last time, to the old home place.

Things didn't turn out that way.

The first derailment of her plans happened two miles north, where the road veered right and ran parallel to Rooster Creek. She knew that she would soon be able to see the house in the distance. Katie soldiered on, trying not to think about her sore feet and listening to the moaning of the wind in the trees on both sides of the trail. Suddenly she heard a different kind of moaning. Frowning, Katie left the road, following the sounds, and stopped in her tracks. There before her on the creekbank lay a freckled boy of ten or so. Beside him was a cane fishing pole with green stripes painted on it. Twenty feet away, a bay horse stood tied to a sapling.

The boy's eyes opened for a moment and focused on her, and he mumbled the word "rattlesnake." Then she noticed the boy's left hand, swollen to twice its size. A closer look revealed, at the bottom of his thumb, two fierce red spots.

Katie dropped her bag, ran to the horse, and untied him. If he hadn't been saddled and gentle, she thought, or if the boy had been bigger, all this would've been over before it started—but somehow she was able to boost the groggy child up into the saddle and then climb up behind him. Holding him tight in front of her, she steered the horse back to the road and paused a moment. Her former home was about a mile away, to the right—but what good would that do? She jerked the reins to the left, dug both heels into the horse's flanks, and headed for town.

By the time they arrived the child was out cold, and slumped forward so far she could barely hold him in the saddle. A woman in a yellow bonnet saw them coming, hurried into the street to meet them, and directed Katie to the office of the town doctor, who helped her get the boy off the horse and inside. Twenty minutes later the doc looked at her over his glasses (she was reminded of the clerk at the stage office) and said, to her vast relief, "He'll be all right."

She asked, as the thought occurred to her, "Does he have somebody to take care of him?"

"I've already sent someone to fetch his mother. His pa's out of town." The doc studied her gravely. "Good thing you brought him in. Must've been a giant of a rattler, for a bite that size. You saved this boy's life."

It was the first time she'd thought of that, and the realization jarred her a bit. Before she could reply, though, she remembered her bag, and the money inside. It wasn't a lot but it was all she had. Without a word Katie fled the office and flew back up the street. Minutes earlier a passing shower had muddied the road and her feet were blistered and aching, but Katie Harrison had endured worse. At least the clouds kept the heat from being too bad.

What *was* bad was that when she arrived at the spot where she'd found the boy, her bag was gone. Even the fishing pole was missing. She stood there a moment, alone on the creekbank, her breath rasping in her throat.

Finally the tears came. Katie staggered backward against the trunk of a sweetgum and slowly slid down it to the ground. She knew she shouldn't be surprised; life had never been kind to her—her parents being forced to sell their home and move back to Alabama, her pa passing away soon afterward, and her older sister leaving last year, leaving Katie to care for their dying mother—but the idea that she had stopped here to help a person in need, only to have someone come along and steal all her earthly possessions ... well, that was hard to take.

After several minutes of self-pity Katie drew a huge, hitching breath, let it out, wiped her eyes, and rose to her feet. She had two choices: head back to town or keep going. She pushed on.

As she trudged along the dirt path it occurred to her that she didn't even know the name of the boy she'd rescued. Not that it mattered. What mattered was that he was all right now, and safe. She had forgotten how dangerous the plains could be. She sharpened her eyes, watching the ground in front of her and to both sides of the trail.

Soon she topped a rise and saw the farm. It looked almost the same, just a few more outbuildings and a fancy porch across the front of the house. This had been her world years ago, and she felt new tears stinging her eyes. As she set out toward the house she saw something else: a horse-drawn wagon lumbering in from a pasture to the west. They crossed paths fifty yards from the house, and she stopped and looked up at the driver, a big black man with a floppy hat. He stopped also. "Where'd *you* come from?" he said.

She thought it was probably obvious, but answered, "Town." Suddenly aware of her puffy eyes and the mud on her dress, she added, "I ran into some trouble on the road."

"You all right?" He seemed truly concerned, and in that instant she knew she liked him.

"I'm fine. Do you work here?"

He snorted. "I'm 'bout the only one who *does* work, here." He jerked a thumb and said, "Hop in. I'll give you a ride to the house."

Katie climbed up and sat beside him on the wooden seat, and he clicked his tongue to the bony horse in the traces. She hadn't realized how tired she was.

"Who lives here, now?" she asked.

"Now?"

She nodded at the house ahead. "I grew up here. Long time ago."

"You a Harrison?"

"Yes. Did you know my folks?"

"Know the name, is all." He stuck out a hand the size of a dinner plate. "Booley Jones."

"Katherine," she said, shaking his hand. "Call me Katie."

"I'll call you Missy, how's that?"

"Who owns the place, now?" she asked again. "My folks had to sell it to the railroad."

Booley Jones's coal-black face hardened. "Railroad never got built through here. Owners are Mr. and Miz Carter. Jesse and Maureen, though I don't call 'em that. They been here maybe five years."

"Are they old? Young? Do they have a family?"

"They 'bout my age," he said, which wasn't much of a hint. Booley Jones could've been anything from forty to sixty. "And no chillun. It's just the two of 'em."

"You don't seem to like them much."

"I work for 'em," he said, which again clarified nothing.

By now they were near the front steps. He hauled the wagon to a stop, and Katie jumped down. "Pleased to meet you, Mr. Jones."

"Booley." He touched the brim of his hat, jiggled the reins, and rumbled away.

Katie stood there a moment, studying the new porch, the chairs lined up across it—one of them so high-backed and padded it looked like a throne—and the closed and somehow forbidding front door. All of a sudden this didn't seem anything like her old home.

* * * *

The woman who answered the door looked out of place also. She was tall, pale, dressed in black from throat to ankles, and had the flat, dark eyes of a lizard. Her hair, pulled back into a bun, was as blood-red as a desert sunset. She fixed Katie with a cold gaze and said nothing at all.

Katie stood in the doorway, swallowed, and told the same story she'd told Booley Jones, plus a little more: this used to be her home, she was on her way west to live with her sister, and she'd wanted to stop and look at the place one last time. Would that be all right?

"Fine," the woman said. "Just walk backward as you leave, and look all you want."

For a moment Katie was too stunned to reply. This was the last straw. The failure to find a buggy, the long walk, the discovery of the snakebit child, the frantic ride back to town with him, the theft of her belongings … and now this?

For the second time that afternoon, she broke down in tears.

"Oh, for God's sake," the woman said. She grabbed Katie's elbow in a claw-like grip, led her to a chair in the entranceway, pushed her into it, and stood looking down at her.

Katie wiped at her eyes with her sleeve, hating herself for acting this way but unable to stop blubbering.

"Mrs. Carter doesn't have much patience for this kind of thing," the woman said, "but she finds herself curious as to why you're carrying on this way."

Sniffling and hiccupping, Katie said, "I don't really know. I just— I've lost what little money I was carrying…and now I don't know what to do. Walk back to Perdition, I guess, try to find work. I have to earn enough for another stagecoach ticket."

Silence. Finally the woman said, "Mrs. Carter might have another way."

"I thought you *were* Mrs. Carter. You're not?"

"I am. But Mrs. Carter doesn't care for questions," the woman said stiffly, "unless she's the one asking them." She paused and added, "Are you interested in hearing her proposal?"

Katie nodded. She thought that might be the safest response.

"Can you cook?" the woman asked.

"Yes ma'am."

"What can you cook?"

"Most anything."

The dark look remained. "We lost our cook a month ago. Mrs.

Carter doesn't like to cook, her husband doesn't know how, and that ignorant helper we have—Mrs. Carter saw you with him in the wagon—goes home to eat with his ignorant family. So here's the offer: you fix and serve our meals, and in return you get room and board and a fair wage. Yes or no?"

"Yes," Katie said. Did she have a choice?

"One more thing. Mrs. Carter doesn't like you much. You better hope she likes your cooking. If so, you can stay until you earn your passage west. Agreed?"

"Yes ma'am."

"Your quarters will be in the barn. You can take your things there."

"I have no things."

The tall woman gave her a why-am-I-not-surprised? look, then pointed to a doorway. "There's the kitchen. We eat at seven o'clock."

* * * *

Supper was indeed ready at seven, and was served by a brand-new Katie Harrison, one who had scrubbed away the mud and changed clothes. She now wore a pink dress that fit surprisingly well. No explanations had accompanied the loan of the dress, which was far too small and colorful for Mrs. Carter to have worn, and Katie had asked her no questions.

The meal she prepared was simple but delicious, and although Mrs. Carter said no words of approval, she also said nothing negative. She just sat alone at the huge gleaming table in the dining room, ate every bite, and then stomped up the tall staircase to—Katie assumed—her bedroom. Katie ate at the kitchen table. Afterward, as she was washing the dishes, she turned to see Booley Jones standing just outside the screen door. He was hatless now, and wore clean overalls and a white shirt. Katie jumped and almost dropped a bowl.

The big man held up both palms. "Sorry, Missy. Didn't mean to sneak up on you. You dern sure don't want to drop nothin'."

"What is it?" she asked, heart still pounding. "Is something wrong?"

"I live down that way," he said, pointing into the darkness. "And I got a telescope a soldier give me, once. I been watchin' awhile, seen you bustlin' about. I figured she musta hired you to cook." He studied her a minute. "That's Izzy's dress, ain't it?"

"Izzy?"

"Isabelle Watson. She was the cook, till just awhile back."

Katie found herself looking down at the pink dress. "Mrs. Carter let me borrow it. Why would she still have the cook's dress?"

Booley shrugged. "Don't know."

"You still haven't told me why you're here. Is anything—"

Boards creaked above their heads, then Katie heard a door squeak open and the clomp of shoes on stairs. In a flash Booley Jones stepped back into the darkness. Thoroughly confused now, Katie turned and resumed her dishwashing.

Moments later Maureen Carter stood in the doorway between the kitchen and dining room. Her face, as always, was expressionless, but her eyes darted everywhere. "Did Mrs. Carter hear voices?" she asked.

Booley's face appeared again, looking embarrassed. "It was me, ma'am. I brought them peas my wife shelled for you. Just stopped to exchange pleasantries."

Mrs. Carter eyed them both a moment, then clomped back up the steps. A door opened and closed, but Katie waited until she heard the boards overhead groaning again before she turned to Booley. "Why does she talk like that?" she asked, whispering this time.

"Like what?"

"You know. Calling herself Mrs. Carter."

"Beats me," he said.

"She gives me the willies." Katie glanced up at the ceiling, then back again.

"Look, I didn't bring no peas. I came here to tell you somethin'," he said. "Two things. First, you be stayin' in the barn, right?"

"Yes. The little room in the corner. I'll be careful with the lantern, if that's your worry."

"It ain't. I wanted you to know I put a latch on the door to that room a minute ago, after I realized you're stayin' on. It'll lock from the inside now, and the padlock and key is under the sleepin' mat. You put that lock through the latch and snap it shut, every night, understand?"

"No—I'm not sure I do understand."

"You just do like I'm tellin' you. I also put an old cowbell under that mat. You ever need to, you ring it, hard. I'm only a little piece down the hill. I'll hear it, and come runnin'. All right?"

"You're scaring me a little here, Booley."

"Can't help it. You do like I say." He frowned. "You ain't met Mr. Carter yet, have you?"

"No. She said he wouldn't be back for a while."

Booley nodded. "He went huntin' this afternoon, down on the

Rooster. Prob'ly went on to town after, and when that happens he stays the night. Comes in drunk the next day." His eyes narrowed. "You stay away from him. You hear him, you go the other way, 'less I'm around."

Katie swallowed and nodded. "I will."

"I hate to worry you, I really do. But I got a daughter myself, and—especially now, seein' you in Izzy's clothes ..."

She nodded again. "I'll be careful. What was the other thing?"

"Ma'am?"

"You said you came here to tell me two things."

"Oh. Just be sure you do what they tell you to do. Don't fuss, don't argue."

He turned then, to leave. She saw, for the first time, that he walked with a limp.

"Booley?" she said. Still whispering, but loud enough he could hear her.

"What?"

"The cook. Isabelle. What happened to her?"

Booley had stopped, but didn't turn around.

"You ring that bell if you need me," he said, and left.

* * * *

The night passed without incident, and breakfast went well: bacon, eggs, fried potatoes, and biscuits for Mrs. Carter, who sat alone at the dining table and ate like a field hand. At the noon meal Katie finally met the master of the house.

Jesse Carter showed up out of nowhere, sitting there across from his wife. Mrs. Carter had already told Katie to cook a big enough meal for two, but did nothing else to prepare her for her first sight of the mysterious husband. He was an odd-looking man: thin face, big ears, long hair slicked back with enough pomade to grease a whole set of wagon wheels. His eyes looked tired and bloodshot, which—from what Booley had said, about his habits—didn't surprise Katie much. What did surprise her, and alarmed her too, was how creepy those eyes were. They watched her every second she was in the room. She now understood Booley's warning.

Actually, avoiding Jesse Carter wasn't hard. He was often gone, and when he was around he was loud and lumbering. Katie became an expert at keeping out of his way. She did her job three times a day, locked herself into her room in the barn at night, and kept a careful record of how many days had passed and how many yet-to-be-received dollars had been earned. If her calculations were correct, she could be out of here in two months.

* * * *

Only once did Katie see the second floor of her childhood home. She was in the kitchen one afternoon, chopping vegetables for a stew, when Maureen Carter strode in from the porch and ordered Katie to go upstairs and bring her pearl necklace down from her dresser.

"Which room?" Katie asked.

"Top of the steps, turn right. The door's open. And make it fast."

"Yes, ma'am." That was her parents' old bedroom.

But Katie couldn't find the necklace. Several expensive-looking pieces of jewelry littered the top of the dresser, but no pearls. She picked up a gold-plated jewelry box the size of a brick and brought it down instead. Surely the necklace would be inside.

As soon as Mrs. Carter saw her, the older woman's eyes almost popped from her head. "*Give me that!*" she shrieked, snatching the jewelry box from Katie's hands.

"This is not what Mrs. Carter asked for," she said, in an icy voice. Then, leaning forward until she was almost nose-to-nose with Katie, she said, "Did you open this box?"

"No, ma'am. I thought—"

"Stupid girl," Mrs. Carter muttered, and whirled around to mount the stairs. "Mrs. Carter will get it herself."

"Fine with me," Katie whispered to her back. As Katie retreated to the kitchen, she noticed Booley outside the back door, staring at her with raised eyebrows. She shrugged in reply, and he nodded. The look on his face was clear: just another day in the loony bin.

* * * *

On a sunny morning two weeks into her employment Katie spent an hour picking pole beans in a neatly-hoed patch down the hill from the house. On the way back she spotted Booley in a grove of cotton-woods. She headed that way and found him sitting motionless on the near bank of Rooster Creek. Wrapped around his right fist was one end of a fishing line; the other end disappeared below the water's surface. Ten feet away, a cork bobbed in the sluggish current.

She sat down beside him with her sack of beans. "Are they bitin'?" she asked.

"Not *my* bait, they ain't. Whatchoo want, Missy?"

"Just visiting. I bet Mr. Carter has a fishing pole you could borrow, if you wanted to."

"He got plenty of 'em, in the shed. But I ain't borryin' one, and don't you neither. I'm foolin' myself anyway—I ain't never seen a fish in this creek."

She turned and looked over her shoulder at the dirt road, the one she'd walked fifteen days ago, on her way here. "Nobody ever comes here from town," she said. "Do they?"

"I hope they don't, right now. Anybody comes along now, sees a white gal sittin' here talkin' to a black man, they'd prob'ly shoot me dead."

"I'm serious. Nobody *ever* comes here, and she never goes anywhere."

"Ain't no need to, I guess. She sends me to get the mail, fetch supplies and such."

Katie stayed quiet awhile, then said, "Are they both crazy? Is that it?" It still hurt that a place of such wonderful memories was now overseen by those two.

"Don't know 'bout that. Know Miz Carter's got a brother lives in Perdition, a rich brother. She never speaks to him, though, and never sees him."

"Hmm."

"Anythin' else you want to know?"

"Yes. You told me, the other night, to do whatever they say."

"I sho' did."

"Is that what *you* do?"

"Always," he said.

"Anything they tell you?"

"Yep. And keep your voice down."

"Why? Mr. Carter's gone, and she's in the house."

"I mean the fish. Talkin' scares 'em off."

"Oh. Right. The ones that aren't there." Suddenly she felt a deep sadness. In a whisper she said, "Why do you do it?"

"Do what?"

"Why do you stay here, Booley? They think you're a fool, and you let them think that. And you already said you do whatever they tell you. Why?"

Booley Jones sighed, long and deep. "I'm gettin' old, Missy. I'm half crippled, and got a sick wife and a young 'un who depend on me. Work's hard to find, and while I ain't sayin' I like it here, I get paid and paid good. Result of all that is, if they say jump, I jump. And till you earn enough to get yoself outa here, I advise you to jump too."

"But what if it's something bad?"

"What?"

"What if one of them tells you to do something that's bad, or wrong? What then?"

He shrugged his huge shoulders. "Comes down to it, I'll do whatever I have to, for my family."

A silence passed. Then: "Another question. Isabelle, the cook."

"What about her?"

"What was she like?" Katie asked.

"Just a young gal, like you. Kind to me, like you. Purty yellow hair, green eyes, wore a little silver bracelet with charms on it."

"Did she leave because of Mr. Carter?"

"I told you, I don't know nothin' bout why she left, or how. One day she was just gone."

"But he looked at her funny, didn't he? Mr. Carter, I mean."

Booley stayed quiet, frowning. "She didn't like him—that's all I know."

"And there was no lock on *her* door, in the barn. Was there."

"No," he said.

* * * *

The very next afternoon someone *did* come up the road from town. The first Katie saw of him was at supper, at the table with the Carters. His name was Clay Wallace, a tall man in his early thirties with curly hair and a bright smile, and he introduced himself as a representative for the Colt Firearms company. Which meant, she supposed, he was a salesman. Jesse Carter had apparently ordered some pistols and Wallace stopped to deliver them on his way to Dodge City. After supper Katie could hear him and Mr. Carter talking in the living room, and when she later retired to her pallet in the barn she couldn't help thinking about him.

The next morning she heard pops of gunfire from behind the house, and through the kitchen window she saw the two men shooting at targets. Once, when she was fetching water from the well, Clay Wallace turned and looked at her, and they both smiled. The silent exchange of glances continued at lunchtime and supper. That night after Mrs. Carter had gone upstairs and while Mr. Carter made a trip to the outhouse, the gun salesman eased into the kitchen, turned her gently around from her dishpan, and stole a kiss.

"What in the world," he whispered, holding her as her hands dripped dishwater on his shoulders, "is someone like you doing out here?"

"Waiting for you," she said, clutching him fiercely. Only later would she wonder why she'd said something so stupid.

Clay Wallace apparently didn't think it was stupid. He stayed another full day, and they secretly met twice more—once in the kitchen the next morning before the Carters were up and about, and once the next night, in her quarters. They swapped life stories, and after she had told him about the half-dead boy she'd found by the creek—the first time she'd told anybody about that—Clay slipped a small one-shot pistol into the pocket of her apron.

"Keep it with you always," he said. "In a pocket, or tie it to your leg under your dress if you have to. It wouldn't kill a bear but it'd kill a rattler. If you got close enough."

She was flabbergasted. "I can't take this."

"Consider it a loan," he said, before kissing her again. "I'm becoming a man of means. Jesse Carter's already bought three revolvers from me and he'll probably buy more."

"So you'll be back?" He'd said he was going to Dodge from here.

"I'll be back, whether he buys anything else or not. Two or three weeks at the most."

"You promise?"

"I promise."

Clay Wallace left at sunup the following morning, turning twice in his saddle to look back as he rode away. The Carters didn't come out to see him off—even if they'd been out of bed, they were not farewell-bidders—but Katie stood on the porch and watched the tall rider until he waved and rounded the last bend, down near the Rooster. As she turned away she saw Booley Jones watching too, off to one side of the porch.

"He told me he'd come back," she said to him, wiping away a tear. "You think he will?"

Booley sighed. "I doubt it, Missy. But for yo sake, I hope he does."

She knew what he meant. Disappointment was nothing new to either of them.

* * * *

The days passed. Booley Jones chopped wood and tended the

fields and fished in the creek where there were no fish, Maureen Carter sat regally on her huge chair on the front porch and did whatever it was that she did upstairs, her husband hunted and drank and played with his new guns and spent a lot of nights in town, and Katie cooked and cleaned and kept a wary eye on Jesse Carter. She still dreamed of leaving, but mostly she dreamed of Clay Wallace.

Thirteen days after he'd left, Katie's homemade calendar told her it was payday. When the breakfast dishes had been finished she gathered her courage and hurried out to see Mrs. Carter, who was already perched on her ridiculous throne on the porch, silently regarding her fiefdom. Although Katie was standing, the chair was so tall the two women faced each other at eye level.

"I believe I'm due a month's wages," Katie said, her voice high but steady.

Maureen Carter looked at her as if she were a frog in her soup, but—surprisingly—rose from her chair and walked to the front door. "Stay," she said to Katie, and went inside. Moments later she reappeared with a handful of bills, counted them one by one into Katie's palm, and without another word took her seat and resumed staring into the distance. That was quite all right with Katie. She took the money and headed for her room in the barn.

Halfway there she stopped dead. One of the bills she'd been given had a red heart-shaped smudge on a top corner; a drop of paint maybe, or dried blood. Either way, she'd seen it before.

This was one of the bills from her travel bag. The bag that was taken, that day on the bank of Rooster Creek.

Could she be mistaken? She looked again, closely. No. It was the same bill. Even as her face grew warm, as her jaw tightened so hard her teeth hurt, she thought of something else to check. Turning left, she headed not to the barn but to the equipment shed, the one where Jesse Carter kept his sporting gear. She threw open the door, stepped in, and looked around: tackle boxes, fish stringers, traps, knives, saddles, lassos, workboots, rifle scabbards, a hundred other items. And off to the right, propped against a corner, there it was. A cane fishing pole with a green-striped handle. The pole that had been lying beside the snakebit boy—beside the bag she'd left behind that day—on the creekbank.

It made sense. She remembered Booley telling her that Jesse Carter had been hunting that afternoon, down on the Rooster. He must've taken her bag, and this pole, while she was away in town with the boy. Not a criminal act, in itself; no one had been around to claim them. But

Katie's name had been on the bag, and on some of her belongings inside. He and Mrs. Carter hadn't known her name then, but they knew it after she'd arrived and started working here. They knew the bag—and the money—was hers. They'd known it all along.

She heard a sound, and backed out of the shed. Twenty yards away, in the dusty shade of the barn, Jesse Carter was saddling his horse, probably for another hunting trip. He was facing the other way, muttering to himself.

For possibly the first time in her life, Katie Harrison didn't stop to think, or plan, or reason. Furious, she marched straight to Carter and blurted, "You took my money."

He turned and regarded her calmly. "I what?"

With a trembling hand she held up the stained bill. "Mrs. Carter just gave me this. It was in the traveling bag I lost on my way here. *My* bag, with my name on it." Her voice cracked with rage, but she didn't care.

He was smiling, his eyes flashing. "Is that so." He dropped the saddle strap and moved toward her slowly, hands loose at his sides, his smile more of a sneer now. "What do you plan to do about it?"

"I plan to have you give me back what you took from me," she said, breathing hard.

"I think you need to be taught a lesson," he said. "The same way Isabelle did."

That stopped her. *Isabelle?*

"You look a lot like her, in that dress."

Katie gaped at him, her heart thudding, ears roaring. How could she have been so stupid? Of course they'd kept Isabelle's clothes. Isabelle didn't need them anymore.

"You killed her," Katie said, amazed that she hadn't seen it sooner. "Didn't you."

"I'll kill you too, girly, if you don't do what I say." He ran a hand through his greasy hair and pointed. "Get in that barn."

Katie swallowed. The anger was still there, blazing in her heart, but terror overtook it. *Stay away from him*, Booley had said. And what had she done, instead? Provoked him.

She didn't have time to think. In a blink he grabbed her by the hair and threw her into the barn. She landed on her back, hard, and he leaped on top of her. One of his hands gripped her neck like a vise, shutting off her air; his stinking breath was hot in her face.

Her vision was blurring, white dots winking in the blackness. She was about to die. As if in slow motion, her right hand moved up her side, then reached past his shoulder, to his neck. Fighting the pain, she squeezed her eyes shut, groped upward still further with the little pistol Clay Wallace had given her, jammed it into Carter's left ear—

And pulled the trigger.

* * * *

That was three hours ago. Jesse Carter was stone dead now, and probably one of the most surprised folks ever to arrive in Hell. And here Katie was, standing in a dress soaked with his blood on a rickety straight-backed chair underneath an oak tree at just past noon, on a hill two hundred yards from her childhood home, with a noose around her neck.

She could only vaguely remember Maureen Carter's screams, and Booley's strong hands heaving the body off her and then lifting her gently to her feet. It didn't take Mrs. Carter long to calm down, though, and when she did she ordered Booley to tie Katie's wrists behind her, gather up a rope, a chain, and the little wooden chair he'd once used for a too-tall milking stool, and drag her to the hill where they now stood. Then the two women waited there while Booley went back to fetch Mrs. Carter's heavy thronelike chair from the front porch. There she now sat, the Evil Queen of the Plains, glaring at Katie with eyes as black as death. Beside her, Booley Jones stood waiting, ever ready to do whatever he was told. How Katie remembered those words.

Katie knew, although she could no longer see it, that one end of the chain Booley had brought was looped around a front leg of her chair. The other end lay on the grass in front of her. The slightest pull would upend the chair.

"Such a shame," Maureen Carter said, breaking the silence. "Such a short, pitiful life you have lived." She paused, as if thinking, and added, "Just like Isabelle."

Mrs. Carter knew about that? Katie didn't reply. What did it matter now?

After a long pause, Maureen Carter said, "Pick up the chain, Booley."

Booley Jones turned to look at her.

"Pick it up, and wait for Mrs. Carter's command."

He limped forward until he was standing three feet from Katie's chair. He looked down at the end of the chain lying at his feet.

Katie hardly noticed him. She was thinking about Isabelle the cook, and Maureen Carter, and the gold jewelry box on the dresser in the upstairs bedroom.

"Isabelle's bracelet," Katie said to her. "It's in that jewelry box. Isn't it."

Mrs. Carter didn't respond. A tiny smile appeared on her lips.

Again she said to Booley, "Pick it up."

Booley drew a long breath, let it out. Somewhere in the distance, a bird called, a strangely beautiful sound. The wind whispered in the oak leaves overhead.

"Booley? *Pick up the chain.*"

"No," he said.

Another silence. Finally Mrs. Carter, her face reddening, rose from her chair, stomped over to them, gave Booley a withering look, and said, "Move out of Mrs. Carter's way."

Booley took a step back, his eyes fixed on Katie. Maureen Carter turned to her also, grinned savagely, and stooped down. One hand reached for the chain, the other was balled into a fist. What Mrs. Carter didn't see—but Katie did, from the corner of an eye—was that Booley had made a fist also, a fist as big as a cantaloupe. As Mrs. Carter straightened up again holding the chain, glaring at Katie in triumph, Booley Jones reached high and brought his fist down on the top of her head with a sound like a hay bale dropping from a barn loft. Maureen Carter's eyes, so fierce and hateful a second earlier, went as blank as marbles. The chain slipped from her fingers, her mouth sagged open, and she fell dead.

But she also fell onto the chair. Unsteady to begin with, the two rear legs snapped like dry twigs. Katie heard, from somewhere, a flurry of gunshots, close together like fireworks—was someone shooting at her? If so, that didn't matter a bit, now. Her last conscious, frantic thought was that she longer had anything to stand on.

She was falling.

* * * *

Her eyes opened to see Booley Jones kneeling over her, cradling her head in his giant, leather-tough hands. She was lying on her back on the hard ground. Katie raised her fingers to her neck, felt the rough noose still there. But she was—somehow—still alive.

"You caught me," she whispered.

Booley shook his head. "You fell back'ards, away from me. I fell down too—she bounced off the chair and landed on my bad leg. You just fainted."

"But ... how—"

Booley's head turned to the left. She followed his gaze. In the distance, Clay Wallace walked toward them from the trees. In his hand was a long rifle. Vaguely she remembered the shots she'd heard, as she fell. Flat, sharp cracks. Rifle shots.

She turned again, looked up and past Booley, past his gentle, worried face, looked straight up at the tree. The limb where the rope had been tied was torn and pitted, fresh wood gleaming through the bark.

"He cut the rope," Booley said. "I never saw nothin' like it. Shots near bout tore the limb in two."

She focused on Clay, standing above her now, leaning forward, his forehead wrinkled.

"I thought you just sold pistols," she murmured.

"I do. Want to buy one?"

She felt herself smile. Her fingers touched the noose again, so Booley loosened it and slipped it off. The two men helped her sit up. With tears in her eyes, she pulled them both to her and hugged them tight. Then she gave Clay a long look.

"You came back," she said.

He nodded. "I told you I would."

* * * *

At five o'clock that afternoon, Katie Harrison stumbled out the front door, rubbed her eyes with her knuckles like a little girl, and slumped into the closest rocking chair. Clay Wallace was already there, sitting on the porch rail.

"You all right?" he asked.

"I'm fine." Except for the skin on my wrists and neck, she thought. "Why didn't you wake me?"

"Figured you needed to rest awhile."

She looked around. Mrs. Carter's throne was noticeably missing; its absence reminded Katie all too well of today's events. "When are we going to report what happened?"

"Already did. Booley and I rode into town while you were nappin'. Took both bodies with us in the wagon, talked to the sheriff for an hour. There'll be no charges."

"But ... I killed someone today, Clay. So did Booley. Won't there be an investigation?"

"Jesse Carter's death was self-defense—Booley saw him try to choke you—and Jesse's wife was about to kill you, too. Besides, Booley and I found Isabelle Watson's silver bracelet right where he heard you say it'd be, in Mrs. Carter's jewelry box. We don't have Isabelle's body, but we told the sheriff what you told us Jesse said, about murdering her. The Carters were not well thought of in Perdition. He believes you."

Katie sat there, mulling it over. Finally she looked around again. "Where *is* Booley?"

"He and his family are getting their things together. That place he's living in isn't his, you know. It was the Carters'."

She closed her eyes and shook her head, remembering the hanging tree, the chair, the chain. "What'll he do now? I'm grateful to be alive, but he and I are both out of a job."

Before Clay could reply, they heard a horse whinny, and looked up to see a lone rider approaching from the direction of town. A man Katie had never seen before trotted a dappled white mare up near the porch steps and stopped there, forearms resting on the saddle horn.

"Miss Katherine Harrison?" he asked. When she nodded, he said to Clay, "You must be Mr. Wallace."

"And you," Clay said, "must've been talking to the sheriff."

"Indeed I have been." The stranger swung down off the horse, tied her to the porch railing, and stuck out a hand. "My name's Lawrence Mayfield. I own the Bank of Perdition."

They shook hands all around, and Mayfield took a seat with them on the porch.

"What brings you out here?" Katie asked him.

"Ownership of this property," he said. "Maureen Carter was my sister."

Katie and Clay gaped at him. She vaguely remembered Booley telling her there was a wealthy brother in town. "I'm sorry," was all she could think of to say.

Mayfield held up a hand. "I'm not here to make trouble. This was a tragedy, but from what I've heard—and believe me, I knew my sister and brother-in-law—you did what you had to."

Katie hesitated, then said, "We'll be leaving soon as we clean things up a bit—"

He shook his head. "That's what I came here about. Jesse had no family, and I'm Maureen's only kin, so I now own the place and... well, I wanted to ask if you'd stay on."

"Stay on?"

"Live here. Run the farm. I'd like Booley Jones to stay also. You two could hire some hands, buy some cattle—there's plenty of grazing land in the north section. We could turn a good profit. I'd finance everything, and pay you both well."

Katie suddenly realized her mouth was hanging open. "I—don't know what to say."

Mayfield shrugged. "Say you'll do it."

"Of course I'll do it. At least for a while …" She looked at Clay, and saw the answer in his face. Whatever future they had together, they could still have.

"Good," Mayfield said.

Then Katie's eyes narrowed. "Hold on. We've never even met, you and I. Why are you doing me this huge favor?"

Mayfield studied her a moment, his face kindly but solemn. Then he turned to the cottonwood grove beside the road and called, "Thomas!"

Katie looked too, and saw a small man on a bay horse emerge from the trees and lope toward them. As they grew closer, she recognized not only the horse but the rider. Not a man at all, but the boy she'd found on the creekbank the day she'd arrived.

He dismounted and came to stand before her, and on impulse she drew him close and hugged him. He blushed, which made his freckles darken, and grinned from ear to ear.

When she looked up at Mayfield, he was smiling too. She saw bright tears in his eyes. "Thomas is my son, Miss Harrison. I've been looking for you for a month now."

She swallowed hard, and turned again to Thomas. If possible, his smile grew even wider.

"You're the one did *me* a favor," Mayfield said. "Me and his mother."

Katie hugged him as well, and as father and son rode away, Katie stood watching them, one hand on Clay's shoulder and the other clapped over her mouth.

"The sheriff must've told him what I said about that fishing pole, and your money, and they put two and two together," Clay said.

She nodded. "You know something? If I had been able to rent a buggy that day I got here, I'd never have found that boy. He would've died, Mrs. Carter would've turned me away, I wouldn't have met you …" She blinked back tears. "But now—maybe—I'm really home."

Clay smiled. "Maybe Booley is too."

"Let's go tell him," she said.

Hand in hand, they walked around the house and down the dirt track past the shed and barn and the ragged targets Clay and Jesse had fired at, weeks ago. It now seemed like forever.

Behind them, in the slowly-moving waters of the creek underneath the cottonwoods, unseen and unheard, a fish jumped and splashed.

John M. Floyd's short stories have appeared in *The Strand Magazine, AHMM, EQMM, The Saturday Evening Post, Mississippi Noir, Best American Mystery Stories*, and many other publications. John is also a three-time Derringer Award winner, an Edgar nominee, and the author of six collections of short mystery fiction.

DON'T BANK ON IT
Jack Halliday

"What would you like me to do for you today?"

The words hung in space like a birthday balloon. It was my job to puncture it and bring it in for a landing. But my throat was dry, and I was distracted by a thumping sound. I discovered it was the pulse in my neck.

I stared across the marble counter into the eyes of Marilyn Monroe's kid sister. I had never seen this bank teller before but I wouldn't be forgetting her anytime soon. Wide-set brown eyes looked into mine mischievously. Her dishwater blond hair, with even blonder highlights, was piled high atop her head, willy-nilly, and kept in place by a plastic hairband with a unicorn on it.

I came to and slid my deposit toward her.

"Oh, I'm so tired," she said with a yawn. Then she added, with a seductive smile, while her nimble fingers did their duty with the monetary business at hand, "I'd like to get back into bed right now."

"Busy?"

"Not really." She sighed. "I'm normally not at this branch, and I had to be here before opening. The good news is I get off early this afternoon."

"And it *is* Friday," I offered. Her lips, I decided, had been designed by Rembrandt.

I reached for the deposit slip she slid my way. Our fingertips touched, and I tingled to my toenails. Her skin was golden and goddesslike, as though someone had found a way to liquefy sunlight and turn it into a tanning lotion that could double as makeup.

"How do you want it?" she asked, tongue firmly in cheek.

"I, uh, one ten, two fives and five ones," I stammered.

She smiled and counted out the bills, then slid them across the counter. She left her hands there, palms down, after I gathered the cash. Her eyes were absolutely hypnotic.

"So what do you have planned for the weekend?" she asked, innocently now.

"Nothing special; just a little down-time I guess." My artificial smile felt as comfortable as a pair of size nines on size ten feet.

"I hear ya; that's what I need—a lot of down time."

"Don't we all."

She just stood and stared as though she had all the time in the world and I was the only one in it beside her that mattered. I quickly went through my brain's hard drive searching for files on her. I couldn't place her and couldn't account for her attitude toward me.

She took a deep breath, squared her shoulders, and gave me her biggest and brightest smile.

"Can you think of any thing else you'd like me to do for you … right now?"

She looked as innocent as a farmer's daughter, finished with milking the cows and ready to bale hay.

I pursed my lips. "Nothing comes to mind," I lied.

Her smile was wistful, as though I had disappointed her. Had some opportunity—for who knows what—evaporated into the ether of a dull and dreary Friday afternoon?

"Hey, I hope things turn around for you. Have a super weekend, okay?"

"You do the same," she replied, punctuating it with a nod that said, "I did my duty."

Somehow I found the wherewithal to move away from the counter. I could have sworn I felt those dreamy eyes of hers boring holes into my back, leaving behind wounds that would never heal.

With all the strength I could muster I continued on my way toward the garage, away from this ingénue half my age who was offering me, what, a romantic encounter I had never enjoyed nor would ever forget?

Then I forced myself to shrug off the incident as the unfulfilled longings of a middle-aged private detective whose love life had never quite equaled his imagination of it. I was in my car and on the highway in minutes, and in another ten or so I was back in my office. The entire episode had all but dissipated into a momentary encounter that only served to remind me I was, indeed, still emotionally alive.

* * * *

Several weeks later I was sipping coffee, staring mindlessly through my office window at the crowded city below, when my phone rang. It was Paulsen, at the ninth precinct.

"Howie?"

"Last time I looked; what's up, Jim?"

"Somethin' came across my desk and I thought you might be interested."

"Shoot."

"It concerns a money mix-up. A deposit that, well, that didn't quite get deposited in a 'kosher manner.' You with me?"

I felt my forehead wrinkle while a familiar tingle said hello to my lumbar region.

"Go on."

"An Indian Hill resident deposited a gigunda check at the downtown branch of First American Union."

"Where do I come in?"

"The check cleared," he continued, "but the money disappeared—a couple hundred thou."

I whistled. "What are you guys coming up with?"

"That's just it, the old lady isn't satisfied with our pace in finding the teller who waited on her."

"Did she describe her to you?"

There was a pause. Then he coughed and continued.

"Sure did. Apparently, a new kid on the block, not usually assigned to that branch. A blond, brown eyes, mid-twenties, she thinks."

I sighed as I formulated my final question.

"Do you have a name for this teller?"

"Sure do," he said, triumphantly. "Marilyn Baker. But she's in the wind."

I collapsed back into my chair, an old tire, badly in need of repair.

"Interested?" he asked. "The bank is posting a reward."

He had no idea.

Jack Halliday is an author and award-winning screenwriter based in the Midwest. His work has appeared in numerous digital and print magazines. His first fiction collection was published by Wildside Press as their Mystery Double #12. For more information, visit: www.jackhalliday.com

DIXIE QUICKIES
Michael Bracken

The twelve-room Dixie Motel, sandwiched between the Dew Drop Inn and the Rodeo Bar and Grill on the outskirts of Chicken Junction, Texas, did most of its business on Friday and Saturday nights, when inebriated couples were willing to spend as much for a one-hour room rental as they would spend for an entire night the rest of the week. Weekend encounters at the motel were known locally as Dixie Quickies, and Mr. and Mrs. Smith were the most frequent motel guests, occasionally occupying all twelve rooms at the same time. Even Carlos Rodriguez checked-in as Mr. Smith, but the bottle-blonde who checked in with him as Mrs. Smith left behind no clue to her identity other than the cherry-red lipstick imprint of her kiss on the deceased's forehead.

Guests paid cash at the Dixie Motel, and only the first rental of the evening for each room appeared in the official ledger. The owner kept a second set of books to track the additional income, and both the night clerk and the overnight weekend maids were paid in cash. Two maids, both wearing pink-and-white uniforms and neither with green cards, quickly changed the sheets, towels, and other necessities each time a guest checked out. They wore latex gloves to protect themselves from whatever diseases might be lurking in the effluent of the motel's guests.

Maria de Jesus, the younger of the maids, had seen dead bodies before, so she did not scream when she found Rodriguez, and she did not leave her fingerprints on the dead man's black snakeskin wallet when she emptied it of three twenties and a pair of singles before pulling the door closed and walking to the office. She drew Tiny Campella's attention away from the tattered paperback he was reading and said, "Mr. Tiny? Mr. Smith in Room 12, he is dead."

Like most men named Tiny, Campella was anything but. A high school and junior college defensive tackle long past his prime and recently retired after twenty years of government service, he carried even more weight on his six-foot-four-inch frame than he had back then, and when he stood his low-heeled ropers added another inch to his height. With all his weight stuffed into a pink T-shirt with the motel's logo printed on the back, he resembled a walking billboard for Pepto-Bismol. As he shoved the paperback in the left rear pocket of his jeans, he said, "That ain't good."

The motel consisted of two buildings separated by an asphalt parking lot. One building housed the office and guest rooms one through six while the other housed the laundry and guest rooms seven through twelve. Even though the motel parking lot was rarely full on Friday and Saturday night because most of the guests walked over from one of the adjacent nightclubs, employees parked on the hardpan beyond the buildings, leaving the paved lot for the guests who did drive.

Maria's white running shoes squeaked ahead of him as Campella followed her past the four cars on the lot back to Room 12. She opened the door, showed him the body, and said, "His name is Carlos Rodriguez."

Campella looked down at the diminutive maid. "You know him?"

Maria shrugged, not willing to admit she'd cleaned out the dead man's wallet.

Like any good cowboy, Rodriguez had died with his boots on. He was, in fact, fully dressed for an evening out in a white three-point-yoke snap-button western shirt, dark-wash denim jeans held in place by a wide black leather belt with large oval silver buckle, and black high-heeled, needle-pointed cowboy boots embellished with a snake-skin pattern and silver boot tips. He had shaved earlier that day, his finger-length black hair had been slicked back, and his strong hands displayed evidence of a recent manicure. Rodriguez appeared as if he had sat on the side of the bed, died, and fallen backward. There was no indication that anything untoward had happened in the room, and a quick once-over revealed no obvious trauma to the dead man's body.

Campella had been hired as nightshift clerk to keep trouble away from the motel, and more than once his size had been sufficient to do just that. Size alone would not resolve the current problem, so he stepped outside, grabbed a pair of latex gloves from Maria's housekeeping cart, and pulled them on. Then he rolled the dead man in the bedspread, hoisted the body over his shoulder, and carried it to the door.

"Anyone out there?"

Maria poked out her head and scanned the parking lot. "No, Mr. Tiny. Nobody."

"Rosanna?" he asked, wanting to know the location of Rosanna

Cuellar, the other weekend night maid.

"In Room 4."

Campella handed Maria his car keys, carried the body around the building to where he had parked his aging Ford LTD alongside the maids' two vehicles, and waited as she opened the trunk. He dumped the body inside, closed the trunk, and took his keys.

While Campella returned to the motel's office, Maria went back to Room 12 and stripped the bed. She replaced the sheets, even though they had not been used, and replaced the spread. While doing so, she found, in the darkness on the far side of the room, a white shantung straw Stetson sporting a rattlesnake skin hatband and an eagle feather. Valuable items found in the rooms were tossed in the lost-and-found box, but she knew the Stetson's owner would not be returning for this hat, and she knew a young man living down the street from her who had lost his during the trip up from Mexico a few weeks earlier. So, she stuck the Stetson on her housekeeping cart to take home at the end of her shift.

Less than thirty minutes after Maria discovered the body, a new couple who also registered as Mr. and Mrs. Smith occupied Room 12. Maria changed the room's sheets three more times before sunrise.

* * * *

All the guests had checked out before the motel's owner and the day shift maid arrived to relieve Maria, Rosanna, and Campella. Rosanna drove away first, followed closely by Campella and Maria. Campella turned north, heading past the Rodeo Bar and Grill and away from Chicken Junction. Maria turned south and drove past the Dew Drop Inn, where a lone Ford F-150 occupied the popular bar's parking lot. She drove through the center of town and out the other side to a neighborhood where the residents spoke Spanish more often than English.

Maria considered herself lucky. Many of her neighbors had crossed the Rio Grande seeking a better life and instead wound up working backbreaking twelve-hour shifts for subsistence pay at Chicken Junction's meat processing plant. Though she only worked at the Dixie Motel from eight p.m. Friday night to eight a.m. Saturday morning and the same again Saturday night to Sunday morning, Maria supplemented her income by babysitting the children of the processing plant's nightshift workers the rest of the week. With no taxes deducted from the cash with which they all paid her, Maria's spendable income was sufficient that she did not have to take roommates into her one-bedroom house the way others did.

She stripped out of her pink-and-white uniform and fell into bed. She slept much of the day and rose late that afternoon. After she showered and dressed in a white blouse and blue jeans, Maria collected Carlos Rodriguez's Stetson from her car and went looking for Manuel Ruiz. She found him sitting on the front porch of the house at the end of the block, where he slept four-to-bedroom with his cousin and other men who worked at the meat processing plant. Even though he had his cousin's recommendation, he had not yet been hired.

Despite the glaring Texas sun, Manuel was bare headed. He had lost his hat when he and three other young men were caught in a flash flood while trudging up an arroyo near Redemption. He was lucky that was all he had lost. One of the other young men had died when a white SUV caught in the flood had rolled over him.

"I have this for you," Maria said, offering Manuel the dead man's Stetson.

Manuel settled the cowboy hat atop his head. Though not a perfect fit, he was quite pleased. He smiled, revealing teeth that needed straightening. "*¡Gracias!*"

His smile and the twinkle in his dark brown eyes made her heart race, so she smiled in return. She looked down, scuffed her feet, and asked if he'd had any luck finding work.

"*Todavía no*," he said. "Maybe Monday I start."

"*¿Ha ingerido cena?*"

Manuel shook his head, so she walked with him to the Dairy Queen six blocks away, and paid for their dinner with some of the money she'd lifted from Carlos Rodriguez's wallet. They ate cheeseburgers, split a Blizzard, and reminisced about their mothers' cooking. They had come from different parts of Mexico but shared the same dream— a better life than the one they left behind—and they discussed all the things they hoped to accomplish in the land of opportunity.

After they ate, Manuel walked Maria home and stood with her on the porch. He stood close as she unlocked her door, and she wondered when she turned to face him if he might try to kiss her. He didn't. He thanked her for dinner and then hurried down the steps. As Maria pushed the door open, she heard tires screech behind her. When she turned, she saw a black SUV skid to stop beside Manuel. Two beefy men wearing dark suits and mirrored sunglasses piled out. *¿Polica? ¿Inmigración?* The shorter one grabbed Manuel while the other one snatched the Stetson from Manuel's head and shoved it in his face.

"Where'd you get the hat, *cholo*?"

"I—" He glanced at Maria, his eyes wide with fear. "I found it."

"You're going to show us where."

They dragged him into the SUV and drove away. Maria had seen similar things happen in her hometown of Xalapa, where the Zetas and Cártel de Jalisco Nueva Generación battled over territory, but never in America. Maria stared at the SUV until it turned the corner and disappeared from sight, and then she looked around. Though she saw a few curtains flutter as if they had been open and then suddenly closed, she saw no one else on the street and none of her neighbors ventured from the houses around her.

She needed to tell someone, but whom could she tell? She was an illegal. So was Manuel. To say anything might jeopardize them both, and the people living around her frowned upon drawing police attention to anything in her neighborhood.

Maria pushed inside, locked the door behind her, and drew the curtains. She peeked out every few minutes until it was time to prepare for work.

* * * *

That night, after parking in the hardpan beyond the motel buildings, Maria walked directly to the office, where Campella sat behind the desk reading an old novel about a New Orleans detective named LaStanza. "Mr. Tiny—"

Campella closed his paperback, stuffed it in the back pocket of his jeans as he stood, and listened as she told him what had happened to Manuel. When Maria finished, he said, "You gave the dead guy's hat to your boyfriend?"

She nodded.

"He's going to tell them where he got it," Tiny said. "They're going to come for you, and you'll lead them here."

"I—" she started to protest, but she knew he was right. "What do we do?"

"Nothing," Campella said. "There's nothing we can do right now."

"But—"

"Go on," Campella said. "Get to work. It's going to be a long night."

Maria was about to leave through the side door, which would let her out only a few steps from the door to Room 1, when the bell attached to the front door tinkled. She turned.

A bottle-blonde stepped into the office and asked Campella about a room for the night. Dressed for an evening out, not as if she'd been driving any distance, she wore figure-hugging jeans and a sheer blouse that would draw men's attention away from a face more handsome than beautiful. Her cherry-red lipstick matched the polish on her nails, and her boots were nearly the same color. She seemed familiar to Maria, but she wasn't one of their regulars.

Campella told the blonde the motel's room rate and then added, "Per hour."

The blonde looked around as if seeing the motel for the first time. "What kind of place is this?"

"A very popular place," Campella said. "You want a Dixie Quickie or not?"

The blonde seemed unfamiliar with the term but did not question its meaning. Instead, she asked, "Is there somewhere else I might stay the night?"

Campella told her about a motel on the other side of town. Then he added, "If you're willing to drive a bit more this evening, there's a nice place up the road in Quarryville."

"Thanks," the blonde said. "I might just do that."

Maria waited until the blonde drove away and then she returned to the front desk. "Mr. Tiny, that woman was here last night. She was Mrs. Smith."

"So were a lot of women."

"No, no, no," Maria insisted. "She was Mr. Rodriguez's Mrs. Smith. Did you notice her lipstick? It's the same as the kiss on his forehead."

Campella glanced out the window even though the blonde was long gone.

* * * *

The first guests arrived, and soon Maria was too busy to think much about the dead man, the blonde, or the two men wearing mirrored sunglasses, but she did worry about Manuel. She had known him for only two weeks and already she had lost him.

Several hours later, Maria stepped out of Room 11 with an armload of soiled sheets. On the far side of the parking lot, a black SUV sat idling with its lights off. She ducked back into the motel room and watched as one of the men who'd taken Manuel earlier that day dragged Rosanna, the other maid, out of Room 6. Rosanna was cursing at him in two languages.

Maria called the office and Campella answered.

"Mr. Tiny. Mr. Tiny, those two men who took Manuel, they are here and they have Rosanna."

As she listened to Campella, Maria watched the second man climb out of the SUV to help the first.

"Hide," Campella said into her ear. "I'll take care of this."

A moment after dropping the phone, when he barreled out of the office, shouting at the two men to release Rosanna, Maria expected them to release her. They didn't. Campella stopped short when the taller of the two men drew a semi-automatic pistol from a shoulder holster beneath his jacket and pointed it at the desk clerk.

"This ain't none of your concern, lard ass," the man shouted, "so back the fuck up."

Maria watched Campella raise his hands shoulder high, palms forward.

Rosanna continued to cuss and spit and kick as the smaller man wrestled her into the rear seat of the SUV. Once the door closed, the man with the gun slid behind the wheel and they drove away.

Campella waited until the SUV was out of sight before crossing the parking lot.

"I've got to get you out of here," he said as he entered Room 11. "It won't be long before those two goons realize they grabbed the wrong maid."

As she straightened to her full height, he tossed his car keys at her. "Get in the back, on the floor between the seats. There's a blanket there. Pull it over yourself and wait for me."

Maria did as she was told and soon felt as claustrophobic as she had during the ride north in the back of a panel van with two-dozen other undocumented immigrants. Remembering that trip and how scared she had been then, she hyperventilated, and fainted.

* * * *

Some time later Campella tapped on the window and called her name. "Open the door, Maria. We need to get out of here."

She crawled out from under the blanket, saw that he was alone, and unlocked the door.

"Sorry it took so long," Campella said as he climbed into the driver's seat and tossed a box of latex gloves on the seat beside him, "but I couldn't just walk out. I had to get Mr. Carter to come in early."

"What did you tell him?"

"Nothing he believed." He started the car. "Get up front with me."

She slipped out of the back and into the front passenger seat before Campella drove through the motel's parking lot to the street. Just as he had the previous morning, he turned north past the Rodeo Bar and Grill and away from Chicken Junction.

Maria stared out the window at the passing scenery. "Where are we going, Mr. Tiny?"

"We need to know more about Carlos Rodriguez, so we're going to ask him."

Surprised, Maria said, "Ask him? But he is *muertos*. Dead."

"We sure as hell can't ask anyone else, can we?"

She had no idea what to say, so she said nothing.

* * * *

Campella turned off the state highway an hour after leaving town, and he drove another forty-five minutes through increasingly desolate desert scrub on roads of decreasing quality, causing Maria to bounce around on the seat. He finally stopped and said, "Get out."

She wondered if she planned to leave her there. Then he pulled on a pair of latex gloves, climbed out, and walked around the big car. She grabbed a pair of gloves and followed him over a small rise and into the dry arroyo where Campella had dumped Carlos Rodriguez the previous morning.

Coyotes and vultures had been at the body and it didn't look or smell much like a man anymore, but Campella found Rodriguez's wallet unscathed and in another pants pocket a key ring with only three things on it—a Ford ignition key, a house key, and a Swiss Army Knife. As he pocketed the key ring and before he opened the wallet, Campella looked at Maria and asked, "How did you know his name?"

"I—I took his money."

"You took his money and his hat?"

She nodded.

"What about his cellphone? Did he have a cellphone? Did you take that, too?"

"No, Mr. Tiny. Just his money and his hat."

Campella stared at her for a moment before directing her attention to the dead man's black snakeskin wallet, and together they examined the contents. They found a driver's license with a home address in Mertz, an automobile liability insurance card listing a Ford F-150 but no other vehicles, three credit cards, two receipts from self-service gasoline pumps, and a condom. What they didn't find were a debit card, family photos, medical insurance cards, random business cards, handwritten notes, and the other detritus they both expected to find.

While Maria held their small trove of treasures, Campella tore the wallet apart, looking for any secret compartment that might contain additional information about the dead man. He found nothing and dropped the dismantled wallet next to the body.

"We have to take off his boots."

Maria looked at the state of the dead man's legs—the left still attached to his pelvis, the other torn off at the knee and laying several feet away. She made a face. "*¿Por qué?*"

"He must have something that tells us who he really is."

Campella grabbed Rodriguez's left leg, wrestled off the black snakeskin-patterned boot, and found a .45-caliber two-shot Texas Defender strapped to the left ankle. He unholstered the derringer and it disappeared into one of his large hands for a moment before he handed it to Maria. She had learned to shoot as a child but had not held a gun since kneecapping the van driver who assaulted one of the women traveling with her when she came north. As she slipped the derringer and the contents of the dead man's wallet into one pocket of her motel uniform, Campella unstrapped the holster, removed the dead man's sock, and found nothing else but toenails in need of a trim.

He turned his attention to Rodriguez's right leg. When he could not pull the boot free, he held onto the detached lower leg and told Maria to pull on it. She grabbed the heel and tugged. The boot wouldn't budge, so she braced one foot against Campella, pulled harder, and then fell on her backside when the heel broke off.

Something that had been hidden inside the hollowed-out heel tumbled to the ground between them. Campella realized what it was and stomped it to pieces under his own boot heel. He grabbed Maria's wrist and insisted, "We have to go. Right now!"

Once in the car and speeding away, she asked, "What was that?"

"A GPS tracking device," Campella explained as he peeled off the latex gloves he'd been wearing. "Someone wanted to know where that man was at all times, and I'm surprised they haven't already found him."

Maria looked back in the direction of the body, saw the cloud of dust kicked up by Campella's LTD as they rushed toward the state highway, and wondered how anyone within fifty miles could miss their presence in the Texas scrub. She peeled off her gloves and asked, "Where are we going, Mr. Tiny?"

"We can't go back to the Dixie, and I sure as hell can't take you home, so we're going to my place," he said. "Nobody can sneak up on us out there."

They were both silent for several minutes. Then Campella said, "Your boyfriend. You think he sold you out?"

"I only know Manuel for a couple of weeks," Maria said.

"Manuel?"

"Manuel Ruiz, from Santa Rita Del Sotol."

Campella glanced at his passenger. "So, this kid really isn't your boyfriend?"

"I don't know what he is," she said. "He is a boy who needed a hat and a friend in this new country."

* * * *

Maria had never been to Campella's place and, when she saw it, doubted anyone else had ever been there by choice. At the top of a slight rise, at the end of a long private drive that was little more than twin ruts in the dirt, Campella's dilapidated singlewide mobile home rested on concrete blocks, providing an unobstructed view of the scrub for several miles in every direction. He stopped the LTD a few feet from the concrete steps leading up to the mobile home's front door and silenced the engine.

After they climbed out of the car, Campella led the way up the steps and opened the front door. Maria was unable to see around him, but she could hear a woman's voice asking, "Where is he, Mr. Campella?"

The big man hesitated in the doorway with one hand behind his back to stop Maria. "I thought you were headed over to Quarryville for a room. What brought you back?"

"It had to be you," said the woman inside the mobile home. "No one else could have moved the body. No one else would have tried."

"That so?"

Maria stepped into the mobile home as Campella stepped forward. She still couldn't see through him to the woman talking to Campella, but she recognized the blonde's voice from her visit to the Dixie Motel's office the previous evening.

"I know all about you, Mr. Campella. You have quite a colorful background. Does your employer know about it? Your co-workers? You know—" Her voice grew closer as she approached Campella.

"You know, I could find a use for a man like you."

The blonde pressed herself against Campella and wrapped her arms around him. She held a syringe in her right hand and, from behind Campella, Maria watched the blonde try to jam the hypodermic needle into his left buttock. The needle snapped in half when it failed to penetrate the paperback he carried.

When Campella pushed the blonde away, Maria pulled the Texas Defender from her pocket and stepped around the big man. She saw a couch, a recliner, a bookcase crammed full of paperbacks, and the blonde standing near the television set, still grasping the syringe.

"You brought the maid with you?" the blonde asked. "She help you move the body?"

Maria's father had taught her to protect herself, her family, and her friends. She glanced at Tiny and saw the smear of cherry-red lipstick on his cheek where the blonde had kissed him while trying to jab the hypodermic needle in his ass. She raised the derringer and shot.

As the blonde crumpled to the floor, Maria said, "She wanted to hurt you, Mr. Tiny."

"Oh, Jesus," Campella said as he stared down at the dead woman staining his carpet. "What're we going to do with this one?"

He went back to his car for the box of latex gloves and pulled on a pair before he examined the body. Then he checked her pockets, her shoes, and the inside of her bra. He found no identification of any kind, making her more of an enigma than the man he'd dumped the previous morning.

"We have to get her out of here and clean this place up," Campella said.

Maria removed from her pocket the things they had taken from Rodriguez's wallet, and she stuffed it all in the dead woman's back pocket.

She helped Campella wrap the blonde in his shower curtain. Then, while he carried the body out to the trunk of his LTD, Maria began to do what she did best. She cleaned.

Campella cleaned, too, but he concentrated on removing Maria's fingerprints from the Texas Defender. When he finished with the derringer, he took Rodriguez's key ring from his pocket and realized the Swiss Army Knife held a secret. Though it looked like a regular model, with small blade, scissors, and nail file, it also included a USB stick. He removed the knife from the key ring and put the key ring, the derringer, the syringe, and the broken needle he removed from his copy of

The Big Show into the shower curtain with the blonde. Then he walked several hundred yards into the scrub and pushed aside a large rock to reveal a lockbox containing mementos of his past life. He added the knife to the other contents and returned to the mobile home to find Maria standing on the porch with her arms crossed, watching him.

She told Campella she had watched enough television programs to know her cleaning efforts might pass a cursory inspection, but she also knew they would fail a serious forensics examination.

"Good enough," Campella told her. "Let's go."

* * * *

He drove a different direction, taking her on different roads of decreasing quality through increasingly desolate desert scrub until he reached a ravine he found satisfactory for their purpose.

After he dumped the body and returned to where Maria stood next to the LTD, he said, "I think I need a new car. I'm tired of driving a fucking taxi for dead people."

Maria placed one hand on Campella's arm. "Thank you, Mr. Tiny. I don't know what I would do without you."

"I should thank you," he replied. "I don't know what was in that syringe, but if she had stuck me with it, it might be my body getting dumped out here."

They climbed into Campella's LTD and headed back to the state highway. Long before they reached it, though, they saw a black SUV blocking the dirt road where it intersected with the pavement.

Campella had no real choice. He stopped short of the SUV and waited while the two beefy men in dark suits and mirrored sunglasses pointed handguns at the car and ordered them out and onto the ground.

Campella turned to Maria. "No matter what else you tell them, you tell them I shot the blonde. Do you understand?"

"*Sí.*" She nodded. "Yes."

"Promise me," he insisted.

"Yes."

Then they opened the doors.

* * * *

Twenty-four hours later, after negligible sleep and intense interrogation during which Maria told the truth about everything except who shot the blonde, she was taken to a room where Campella sat. When she saw him in his pink motel T-shirt, her face brightened for the first time since arriving at the non-descript building in San Antonio. She hurried to the empty chair next to his.

The two men in dark suits, neither of whom had ever identified himself to her, settled into chairs on the opposite side of the table.

The taller one said, "Carlos Rodriguez was one of ours, and he'd been undercover for nearly two years. He had worked his way into one of the cartels transporting cocaine and other drugs over the border. When we learned his cover had been blown, we tried to bring him in, but by then we'd lost contact and the tracking device you found and crushed had been non-functional for several months."

Maria looked from the two men to Campella and back. Everything she was hearing was news to her, though it did not appear to surprise Campella. He asked, "And the blonde?"

"You wouldn't have thought it to look at her, but Jennifer Bagwell was known as a breath-taking beauty. The syringe she tried to stab you with contained succinylcholine, a neuromuscular paralytic drug that paralyzes the respiratory muscles so victims stop breathing and asphyxiate."

"That what she used on Carlos Rodriguez?"

"And on three others that we know of. She's also the primary suspect in seventeen other deaths on both sides of the border. That kiss on the forehead is her calling card. The cartel will have to find someone to replace her."

"What about her death?"

"Bagwell was killed with a bullet from Rodriguez's gun," the taller one said. "I'd say that's good enough for him to receive a posthumous commendation."

Campella glanced at the diminutive young Mexican woman sitting beside him before asking, "Where are Manuel Ruiz and Rosanna Cuellar?"

"When we realized they didn't know squat, we gave them one-way tickets home."

"And what about us?" Campella asked.

"Some sources call you a magician because you made so many people disappear in Afghanistan. I don't think anyone up the line wants your name associated with this situation, so you're free to go." He jerked a thumb toward Maria. "This little *puta's* going home with her friends."

Maria looked at Campella. "Mr. Tiny—?"

"That's not acceptable."

"I don't think you're in a position to negotiate."

Campella disagreed and mentioned the USB stick he had taken from Rodriguez's key ring.

When the two agents on the far side of the table glanced at one another, Maria knew Campella had something they wanted, and she began to breathe a little easier.

"When Maria de Jesus gets her citizenship papers, you get Rodriguez's USB stick."

"But that'll take—"

Campella shook his head. "You can have it done in less than forty-eight hours if you really want to," he said. "How bad do you want that stick?"

"Do you know what's on it?"

"I don't know and I don't care, but I'll bet you've torn his place apart searching for it."

The two agents looked at one another a second time and the shorter one nodded.

The one who'd done all of the talking put Campella's keys on the table and slid them across. "We'll contact you in a couple of days."

Campella stood and took Maria's hand. As they exited the building, she said, "Mr. Tiny? What if they say no?"

He looked down at her and smiled. "They won't."

Michael Bracken, recipient of the Edward D. Hoch Memorial Golden Derringer Award for lifetime achievement, is author of several books, including *All White Girls*, and more than 1,200 short stories published in *Alfred Hitchcock's Mystery Magazine*, *Ellery Queen's Mystery Magazine*, and many other publications. He lives and writes in Texas.

FLIGHT TO THE FLIRTY FLAMINGO

Kaye George

Fin watched the door closely. He studied the face of each person who came through. Make that the face of each man. Not many women came to The Flirty Flamingo, except the strippers, and they came in through the alley.

One of the new girls, Jodie Vive, had confided in Fin, as they all eventually did. There was something about him, he knew. People tended to spill their guts. Trouble was, after their troubles were transferred to Fin's admittedly wide shoulders, the weight tended to add up. No one's shoulders were wide enough for all the troubles in this town.

Fin now knew that Jodie Vive's real name was Jory Clark. He supposed her stage name was going for something that sounded like *joie de vivre*, but it missed by quite a bit. He also knew that she was on the run. Lots of the strippers were. They came and went like fireflies, running from abusive men, running back to them, running from drugs, running back to them. Little Jory—now Jodie—was on the run from something heavier still.

A couple nights ago, Jodie—might as well call her what everyone else at Flirty called her—collared Fin at the bar, the end seat, his current favorite. From there he could keep track of the whole room, plus the front door. His girl, Alice, had left for the Ladies' and Jodie took her seat, still warm from Alice's skinny butt. Alice had only warmed part of the stool, though. She was a stunner—brunette, and thin as a rail, light as air. Jodie, on the other hand, had some heft to her. It looked good wrapped around the pole, and that was all that mattered.

"Joe," Jodie muttered, glassy eyes on the bartender. "Need … 'nother one." She swayed on the stool and Fin thought he might have to catch her.

"This is your last, honey." Joe set a gin and tonic in front of her. He and Fin exchanged a private look. Jodie was diving downhill again. She'd done that a few times since she started six months ago. Joe, with

Fin's help, treated all the girls right and made sure the customers did, too. Sometimes they couldn't be helped, but sometimes they could.

"What is it, sweetie?" Fin leaned toward her.

"Someone's after me." Jodie didn't slur that statement. Her eyes looked sharp and sober. "It's someone … from my past."

"Old boyfriend? Ex-husband?"

"'Fraid not. It's worse than that." She remained silent, sipping her drink for so long that Fin thought maybe she *was* as drunk as she looked. She straightened her spine and glanced at Fin. "But I shouldn't involve you. It could be dangerous."

"I've seen danger before, Jodie. A burden shared is a burden lightened."

She smiled. "I've heard you say that a lot. Maybe it's true. Okay. Here it is." One more sip. "A long time ago, back when I was Jory Clark, I was secretary to the governor. I knew he was making dirty deals. I suppose they all do. For most of them, I just turned my head the other way, took dictation and filed. But one day I found something I couldn't ignore."

Fin saw Alice coming out of the restroom and gave her a private signal. She perched on an empty chair and started inspecting her nails. She was used to Fin taking confession from the girls. Alice didn't go on stage, she worked the bar part time. She got close to all the "talent" though, and sometimes let Joe and Fin know when problems were bubbling to the surface.

Jodie stopped for another sip, a long one this time. The canned music that always played between performances floated past them, unheard because so familiar. "It made me sick to see it. The governor was at a fundraising luncheon and he phoned to tell me to get some figures from his office. He wanted to know how much a certain person had donated to his campaign and he kept the figures in a file in his drawer."

"Not a good idea. Those numbers could come back to haunt him."

"He has bigger skeletons than that in his dark closet. Wait 'til you hear. He left his desktop on. I was going through the file when his email inbox pinged. After I gave him the numbers and hung up, I glanced at his screen. The email was from a name I didn't recognize. I read it just in case I should know what it was about. After all, I was his personal secretary. I thought I knew everything about him."

"What's the name?"

"No one you'd know. I hope not, anyway. After I read the email, I forwarded it to my home account and marked his copy *unread*."

"What did it say?"

Jodie shook as a shiver ran through her from head to toe.

"On in five," called Joe.

"I gotta go do my set." Jodie drained her glass and slid off the stool with a thump. "Tell you later."

Alice came over and sat beside Fin. "What was all that, Phineas?" She was about the only person who ever used his given name.

"I'm not sure yet, but Jodie seems to have gotten herself in trouble with the governor."

"Legal problems?" She signaled Joe for another ginger ale, her usual. Fin didn't know how she stayed so thin without drinking diet drinks. She'd been his girl for a few years now. He liked 'em wiry and tough.

"Doesn't seem like it, but I don't know for sure yet."

"You know, there was a guy in here a coupla nights ago watching Jodie's act. I remember him because he stared at her like he could drill right through to the backstage."

"What did he look like?"

"Like a bodyguard. Dark clothes, sat in the corner, quiet, built like a heavy-weight boxer."

"Packing?"

"Probably. He had on a jacket."

Sounded like Jodie was right to be worried. Fin kept an eye out for anyone paying extra attention to her as she swung around the pole, spotlight glinting off the pink spangles in what there was of her costume. No one seemed to be focusing on her. At closing time, he told Alice he'd see her later and walked Jodie to her car. As they entered the parking lot at the back of the building, Fin saw a shadowy figure edge around the far corner of the building. He wanted to take off after it, but didn't want to leave Jodie alone.

"Call me if anything happens," he said as she got into her car.

"I sure will." She slammed her door and sped out of the lot. Fin trotted up the alley to the street and saw her turn at the light. No other cars were on the road and he didn't see any more shadow men. Something was up, though. He'd have to get the rest of that story. Too bad she was in such a hurry to leave tonight.

* * * *

For the next week, he made sure to show up at The Flirty Flamingo on the nights Jodie Vive was on. He studied every customer with his hard, ex-cop eyes. Other than losing a couple hands of poker, nothing bad happened. Alice was away at her mother's for a few days, so he gave his undivided attention to Jodie's problem.

Fin was happy to see Alice when she returned, though, and let her know that in no uncertain terms. Afterward, they sipped brandy together in his bed and he filled her in on what he'd learned from Jodie.

"She says the email was from a guy who must be a pretty dumb jackass. She memorized the email. Said it went something like this— 'The job is done. O'Brien dead. Meet me at the usual place with the money.'"

Alice almost dropped her glass on the duvet. "O'Brien! The guy who was running for governor?"

"Yeah, the guy who died a week before the election, when the gov was losing in the polls."

"Our governor had his opponent killed off?"

"That's what Jodie says. She told me the governor came back from his luncheon after she'd read the email. He came out of his office about fifteen minutes later and asked her what that noise was when they were on the phone. She caught on right away. He'd heard the email come in and knew what time she was in his office. She played dumb and thought he'd never find out she had a copy."

"Did she delete the forwarded email from his *sent* box?"

"She didn't think of that."

Alice shook her head. "They say most crooks are dumb."

"Dumber than bricks. I think this is about a whole truckload of bricks. The killer who sent an email and Jodie who, for a person who works on computers, didn't use even a half a brain. She said she was rattled. The gov must have caught on that she sent the email to herself because he threatened her."

"How?"

"She was vague about that. Maybe he was, too. Anyway, she knew it was time to get out. She packed up and left, changed her name, and got a few jobs around town. Whenever she thought someone recognized her as Jory Clark, she'd fly away again."

"Until she got to The Flirty Flamingo."

"Exactly."

"So ..." Alice examined her glass, the crystal sending weightless sparks to the ceiling from the bed lamp. "What now?"

"Not sure. I'll keep watch and see what happens."

"Are you going to take Bertha to the bar?" Bertha was Alice's name for Fin's Glock. It had been his sidearm when he was on the police force. When he'd left, he gladly quit carrying it. He felt much better without the heavy gun. But he kept it.

"I might."

* * * *

Fin started carrying Bertha and kept watch. Usually he let Joe, the barkeep, handle the rough customers and was only there for unofficial backup.

A week later it broke while he wasn't watching.

It was closing time. Joe was turning out the lights and Jodie, who'd been on that night, was in the back, dressing. Fin heard the shot from his usual barstool. Alice grabbed his forearm, but he shook her off and ran to the dressing area, where the shot had come from.

Jodie stood in the corner, wearing her bra and panties and holding a small pistol. She looked small, but deadly. A man lay on the floor, bleeding from a hole in his chest.

"That's him," Alice said from behind Fin. "The bodyguard boxer guy."

Jodie looked at Alice, puzzled. "He's not a bodyguard. Or a boxer."

"Who is he?" Fin asked softly. Jodie still held the gun. It wavered, sometimes pointing at Fin, sometimes at the guy on the floor.

"I'm FBI," the man on the floor croaked. "This is Jory Clark, the woman who killed O'Brien."

"Shut up," Jodie/Jory shouted and shot at the man, but hit the floor beside him with a whining ping.

"Jory," Fin said, still keeping his voice soft as he drew his Glock from his waistband. "Let's talk about this."

"He's lying," she screamed. "Get out of here, you two. I can handle this."

"I don't think so." Fin took three light steps toward her.

She raised the barrel and fired. She missed Fin.

Alice let out a squeak and Fin heard her fall.

Jory went down with a thud at Fin's first shot. Dead center to the heart. Just like on the shooting range. And like one other time he tried never to think about. Now there would be two.

Fin knelt next to Alice. He took her hand.

"It's just my leg," she said. "It mostly missed." He dropped her hand and felt her leg. She was right. Her wound was superficial.

He put his gun away and turned his attention to the man on the floor. With one hand he pressed on the seeping wound and with the other withdrew the FBI badge from the man's jacket pocket.

"Wish I had my vest on," the man said with a weak grin.

Alice called 9-1-1 and within minutes they heard sirens.

Fin agreed with the agent. "I bet you wish you'd drawn your gun first, too."

"I had no idea she was armed."

"How did you find her?" Fin asked. "She really killed O'Brien?"

"Poisoned him at a dinner where she worked her way in as a server. It's taken a couple of years to gather all the evidence."

"Little" Jory had suckered him, but good. Now who was the dumb brick? "So you came to arrest her without backup?"

"She's a poisoner. I thought she might have pepper spray or something. Never a gun. After we finally tracked her down, I thought this would be an easy collar."

"You don't bring pepper spray to a gun fight," Alice said.

The men both looked at her and nodded.

Fin added the FBI agent to the load of dumb bricks he had mentioned to Alice.

And the weight of one more death to his shoulders.

Kaye George: national-bestselling, multiple-award-winning author of historical, traditional, and cozy mysteries (upcoming: Vintage Sweets series). Her short stories are in anthologies, magazines, her own collection, and her recent anthology of eclipse stories, *Day of The Dark*, by Wildside Press. She reviews for *Suspense Magazine* and lives in Knoxville, Tennessee.

THE ITALIAN TILE MYSTERY

James Holding

Originally published in *Ellery Queen's Mystery Magazine*, September 1961.

It was raining in Positano. The rain bounced off the red-tile roofs, spattered in the gutters of the golden cathedral dome, turned the steep narrow streets into sluiceways. And with the onslaught of the rain all the quaint sunshiny charm that endeared this cliffside village to tourists immediately deserted it, leaving behind an atmosphere of wintry cheerlessness. The pervasive dampness penetrated not only the public rooms of the Savoia Hotel but the very bones of the hotel's guests.

Martin and Helen Leroy sat with King and Carol Danforth in wing chairs before a tiny fire in the lounge. Bundled in bulky sweaters and sports jackets, they stared bleakly through the rain-stippled window to the sullenly breathing Mediterranean below.

"We should have stayed on the *Valhalla*," Helen said, "where it was warm."

"Or the bar of the Excelsior Hotel in Naples," her husband said wistfully. "There's the place to spend a rainy afternoon."

Yet it was this very rain that led Danforth and Leroy into one of the most challenging mysteries they encountered during their cruise around the world on the ship *Valhalla*, now tied up in Naples just a few miles away. The two mystery-story writers (known to their legion of fans by their collaboration team-name of "Leroy King") especially relished the Positano affair because it made more stringent demands on their ingenuity than had even the notable adventure of the African Fish Mystery.

The old-fashioned clock on the wall whirred, preparatory to striking four. Mrs. Cardoni, who owned and managed the small hotel, bustled into the room. She held a large tray before her like an offering. "Tea," she announced cheerfully. "Hot tea. Good for rainy afternoons and depressed people."

They welcomed her. They would have welcomed anything at that point except more rain. "Where will you have it?" Mrs. Cardoni asked.

"Right here in front of the fire," Helen suggested. "Is there a table?"

Her hands being occupied, Mrs. Cardoni pointed with her chin. "There," she said, "by the window."

Leroy rose and went to the window. He lifted a low, tile-topped coffee table and brought it over before the fire. "Just the ticket," he said. "Gather round, people. Put down the free lunch, Mrs. Cardoni, and we'll pitch in. Join us?"

Mrs. Cardoni was pleased. "I hoped you'd ask me," she said. "I brought an extra cup."

Carol Danforth said warmly, "Pour for us, Mrs. Cardoni, please." They liked their landlady very much. She was a plump, amiable widow with a heart as big as her impressive bosom. She treated them, mere guests in her hotel, like members of her own family.

After tea, Mrs. Cardoni removed the tray and Carol Danforth sighed. "Still raining," she said lugubriously. Her eyes passed lightly across the table before her. "My word!" she said. "Look at the table you brought us, Martin."

"What about it?" Leroy asked.

"Take your feet off it for a minute, King," Helen directed, "so we can see all of it."

Danforth, complied.

"Just a tile table, darling," Helen said after giving it a brief glance. "Rather interesting tiles, I'll admit, and quite attractive."

Danforth lit a cigarette. "Charming," he said lazily.

Carol raised a hand to her short dark hair. "I've never seen a more peculiar collection of tiles in my life," she said with more animation than she had exhibited all day.

For the first time, all four really focused their attention on the low coffee table before them. Its top consisted of four rows of tiles, four tiles to a row—sixteen tiles in all—surrounded by a molding of painted wood. Each tile was about six inches wide by nine inches deep, so that the full table top was approximately twenty-four inches by thirty-six inches—two by three feet.

The background color of all the tiles was white and each tile contained a scene or an object obviously hand-painted on the clay before the tile had been given its final ceramic glaze in the kiln.

There was nothing unusual about the construction of the table or its overall decorative effect. Indeed, the white backgrounds of the tiles gave the table top a simple harmonious unity. But when one examined the scenes depicted on the individual tiles, one saw what Carol Danforth meant when she called them a "peculiar collection."

For the pictures seemed to bear no relationship to each other whatsoever. One was of a mountain top; another of a large figure 7 with olive leaves floating across it; a third showed a staff of music; a fourth, a wall with a hole in it. Viewed separately, the sixteen tiles formed a mélange of subjects and colors that might well have been the product of a demented mind.

Danforth stretched his lanky figure in his chair. "This table top could set the tile industry back a thousand years," he remarked.

"It isn't that bad," Leroy protested. The dark eyes in his Indian-like face flashed. "It's an unholy mess in an artistic sense, but it looks pretty attractive at that, just as Helen says."

"Like a wife after you've been married for a while," said Helen with a side glance at her husband. "Usually a mess, but occasionally quite attractive." Helen was blond, statuesque, and lovely. She grinned impishly.

"You're fishing for compliments again," Leroy said. "I wonder who made this table top? It must be unique. There can't be two like it in the whole world."

Mrs. Cardoni passed through the lounge on her way to check on the dinner. Danforth hailed her. "Mrs. Cardoni, we're admiring your beautiful tile table. Where did it come from, if I'm not being impertinent? Is it Italian?"

"In a way," Mrs. Cardoni said, smiling. "It was made right here in Positano especially for me—but by an American gentleman."

Helen said, "We thought some of the pictures on the tiles seemed a little … well, odd."

The landlady flapped her apron with the air of a woman who is about to enjoy a good gossip. "I'll tell you about that table," she said, resting one hip on a chair arm. "One of my guests in the hotel made it. He had a permanent room here for several years until he became ill and died. He was an American like you, but he lived in Italy almost all his life."

"What was his name?" Carol asked. She had a passion for names.

"Lemuel V. Bishop," Mrs. Cardoni replied. She paused a moment, her eyes blank with memory. "His only relative was a brother—a famous lawyer in America, he told me, who did not approve of him because he was an impractical, absent-minded professor who loved Italy more than the United States. He was a lonely man while he lived here at the hotel. He didn't make friends with anybody else, not even the other guests. He'd been a teacher in Ravenna, he said, and now he was old and tired and wished to spend the rest of his life in Positano, where he could see the sea and the golden dome of the cathedral and the fishing boats overturned on the black beach."

They listened sympathetically. "But what about the table?" Leroy prodded gently.

"Oh, yes, the table. After Mr. Bishop became seriously ill, he began to make the table. He got clay and paints and all the materials to make the table itself in the village. And he amused himself for several months up in his room, cutting the tiles and painting them, and putting the table together. He got Giovanni Polito, our local tile maker, to fire his tiles after he'd painted the designs on them."

"But you said he made them for you," Carol said, scenting a faded romance.

"He did. But just as a personal gift for me, because he thought I'd been kind to him while he was sick."

"No wonder he wanted to show his appreciation," Leroy murmured. "It *is* a handsome table."

"I think so, too," she said, "although Mr. Bishop always made a joke about it."

"A joke?" asked Danforth curiously.

"Sometimes I'd go into his room when he was working on his tiles and he'd laugh and say this would be one will his stuffy brother might have trouble reading."

Danforth and Leroy exchanged glances. "You say he called the table a *will*?" King asked.

"Yes. In a joking way. He told me it was his last will and testament, and he was going to leave it with me. And when he died, his brother in America would come and get it." Mrs. Cardoni paused. "He was, of course, joking. No brother ever came."

"How would the brother know he was dead?"

"Mr. Bishop said he wrote his brother a letter several weeks before the end," she explained, "and told him he was dying and that I had his will. And he asked his brother to come here and handle things for him. He also said he told his brother in the letter that he wanted to be buried in Italy—in Ravenna."

"But no brother came."

"No."

"Are you sure he mailed the letter?"

"I mailed it for him myself—airmail. That's when he told me what was in it."

"What did you do when no brother showed up?"

"I used what money he had left to bury him in Ravenna as he asked."

They regarded her in silence for a moment. This was a service above and beyond the call of duty from a hotelkeeper to a guest. Mrs. Cardoni smiled and said. "Mr. Bishop was a fine man. So kind and scholarly and gentle. And a very good guest. He stayed here many months and never complained once about anything. And he always paid his bills promptly."

"Thanks, Mrs. Cardoni," Helen said. "We didn't intend to remind you of what must have been a painful incident. We're sorry."

The *albergatore* waved a hand and rose. "There are all kinds of problems in our trade," she said. "One does one's best." She disappeared into the kitchen.

Carol frowned at her husband and said, "All right, now, darling, I can see the wheels going around in that inquisitive head of yours."

"Why not?" Leroy said. "This could come right out of one of our books, King. A dying man, a will, a stuffy attorney, a kindly innkeeper. Am I right?"

"Completely," his partner said with enthusiasm. "I'll bet Mr. Lemuel V. Bishop wasn't kidding. These screwy pictures on the tiles must mean something."

Carol burst out, "But that's ridiculous! It couldn't be. Or the brother would have arrived to take charge after Mr. Bishop died."

"Ah, my sweet," said Danforth, smiling, "that is exactly where one of my meager talents confirms my guess that there's something to this odd business."

"You mean you've got talent?" his wife asked with a laugh. "I prefer money, darling."

"I just happen," returned Danforth with dignity, "to have total re-call when it comes to news stories, as you very well know. And I distinctly remember that a New York attorney named Clyde R. Bishop was killed two years ago when that big Italian airliner crashed on take-off from Idlewild."

Carol said, "If you remember it, it happened." She turned to Helen. "You see? It's like being married to a computing machine."

Leroy said, "Are you serious, King?"

"Certainly I'm serious. A New York lawyer named Bishop was listed among the fatalities in that crash. See what I'm getting at?"

"That lawyer—Bishop may have been flying *here*, in response to his dying brother's letter, when his plane cracked up and he was killed?"

"Doesn't it fit?"

"Like a suede glove by Barra!" said Leroy enthusiastically.

"And that's why nobody came to read this will?" Helen said, touching the tile table with the point of one dainty shoe.

"Exactly," her husband said. "And that means it probably is a will. And all these months it's just been sitting here in this lounge waiting for someone as brilliant as 'Leroy King' to come along and figure it out, and see that Mr. Bishop's heirs come into their rightful inheritance. Doesn't that sound completely reasonable?"

"It sounds suspiciously like boasting to me," Carol remarked. "But what are we waiting for? Let's get started. I was always a whiz at crossword puzzles."

"Me too," Helen chimed in, "especially on the really tough words like gnu and poi and pyx." She flashed her wonderful smile. "This little old table top shouldn't take us more than a few minutes."

"What we need," said Danforth, "is a system. If the tiles really mean something, we ought to go at the problem scientifically. Don't you think so, Mart?"

"I do. It seems obvious that the tiles must represent words or groups of words. So let's try the simplest system first. Let's write down the words we can think of that best describe each tile."

Helen said, "Shall I be secretary?"

"Please do," said King Danforth gallantly. "I can't imagine a love-lier amanuensis."

"Hey!" Carol interjected. "Why don't you ever say nice things like that to me?"

"You're my wife. And dignified restraint is therefore indicated in my remarks to you." He grinned at his wife and added softly, "At least in public."

Carol flushed. "Come on," she said, "quit stalling. We have work to do."

Leroy said to Helen, "Make a rough sketch of the table top, honey. And number the tiles from one to sixteen. Then identify each tile as we describe it to you. Okay? Tile Number One: a signpost with a hand-shaped sign pointing west. Got it?"

"Got it," Helen said, busily writing. And when Leroy and Danforth had finished describing each tile, her notes looked like this:

1. Hand-shaped sign pointing west	2. Colonial building with sign "The Anchor"	3. Mountain scene	4. Sky and clouds
5. Woman looking at basket on doorstep	6. House on hillside	7. Wall with hole in it	8. Seascape
9. Oil lamp burning	10. Tea cup being emptied	11. Man buckling sword belt	12. Figure 7 with leaves
13. Baby waving	14. Man singing, holding open book	15. Building with egg-crate type walls	16. 8-note scale on musical staff

"Now," said Leroy, "everybody look at tile Number One. And say, in turn, the word or words you think accurately describes the picture on it. This is a *bona fide* brainstorm session, now. We don't want anybody criticizing anybody else's suggestions till we've got them all down. Okay?"

"Okay," said the others in chorus.

"Good. Then you start, Carol."

They looked hard at tile Number One. "Sign," said Carol.

"West," said Danforth.

"Pointing," Helen suggested.

"Left," was Leroy's guess.

Helen wrote the four words down under the proper tile number.

Carol said, "That one sounded like sign language."

They ignored her. "Second tile," Danforth said. "Colonial building with a sign reading 'The Anchor'."

"Inn," said Carol promptly. "Pub."

"Hotel."

"Seamen's rest."

They began to enjoy themselves. Helen wrote the words as they were uttered and before very long Helen's word list looked like this:

1.	2.	3.	4.
sign west pointing left	inn pub hotel seaman's rest	peak hill crag mountain	sky firmament cloud 9 heaven
5. Foundling deserted marketing good Samaritan	6. cliff home Savoia hotel	7. Humpty-Dumpty peek-a-boo aperture opening	8. ocean waves main sea
9. lamp light glow quick	10. grounds dregs good-to-last- drop lees	11. knight sword belt gird	12. Seven Seven Seven Leaves
13. Cheerio bye-bye so long see you later	14. song music singing hymn	15. Hilton school factory hotel	16. octave scale staff do-re-mi

They passed the completed list from hand to hand, studying it, switching their eyes like shuttlecocks back and forth between the listed words and the tiles on the table top.

"Now what?" asked Carol.

"Now," her husband said, "we begin to eliminate. We bring to bear the cool, critical judgment which Leroy King himself displays at all times in his novels. We select the one word for each tile that seems to make the most sense when combined with the others."

"Wait." Leroy was staring at the list. "Maybe we can find a hook to hang our decoding on, if we can figure out why three of these tiles are so similar."

"What's that mean?" Helen asked. "I don't see any tiles that look alike."

"Look at Numbers Two, Six, and Fifteen," Leroy said.

"Bingo!" Danforth said suddenly. "I get it. All three are buildings, and in all three cases one of us suggested the same word to describe them—the word 'hotel.' Right?"

"Right. And Helen even said 'Savoia' to describe tile Number Six—the very hotel in which we are sitting at this moment."

"Sure. But I doubt if the word we want for all three of those tiles is 'hotel.' The sentence in the tiles is probably too short to use 'hotel' in it three times with any significance."

"How about 'inn,' then?" Danforth asked. "Spelled with one 'n' it's a very common word and might easily be used three times in a short sentence."

"Let's try it. Write down the word 'in' opposite tile Numbers Two, Six, and Fifteen, Helen." Helen followed instructions. "That's the only similarity I can see," Danforth proceeded. "So we'll have to assume that each of the other tiles represents a separate word. In which case, what might the first word be, tile Number One, that would make sense coming before the word 'in'?"

Helen looked at her list. "I favor the word 'left' for tile Number One," she said thoughtfully. "It sounds like a word that would be used in a will, don't you think?"

"Not having been left anything by rich relatives, I couldn't say," Leroy grinned. "But if that's your woman's intuition, I'll buy it. First two words, therefore, are 'Left in'."

"We're doing famously," said Danforth. "We're already one-eighth finished."

"I see no reason to bat our brains out on the next two tiles," Leroy said. "In each case only one of the suggested words honestly describes the tiles. So let's put down our first row of tiles to mean: 'Left in mountain sky'."

Helen sucked on her lower lip and looked stubborn. "That's silly," she protested. "'Left in mountain sky'! Is this a new kind of air-conditioned safe deposit vault Mr. Bishop is directing us to?"

"It does seem rather meaningless," Leroy admitted.

At this point Danforth began to display the signs that always portended an announcement of immense importance from him. He cleared his throat, rubbed a hand over his crew-cut briskly, and said, "I think we should all have a drink."

There was no objection to this eminently sensible deduction, so they ordered vodka gimlets all around from Guiseppi, the bartender-waiter of the hotel, who brought the cocktails to them on a classic silver tray that could have come from the ruins of Paestum.

"Now," said Danforth when the first sip of the gimlets had won unanimous approval, "may I parade a little of the perspicacity and analytical skill that, combined with Martin Leroy's, have made us famous?"

"By all means," his wife encouraged. "You look like the cat that has swallowed the cream."

"I must warn you against mixing metaphors, baby," Danforth said. "But no matter. Look at the words we have put down after tiles Four and Twelve. Notice anything about them?"

Silence. Intensive study of the indicated words. Nothing. Leroy said, "Give."

"Gladly," Danforth said grandiloquently. "I shall read them aloud and then, perhaps, the light—"

"Hold it!" Helen exclaimed. "They rhyme! Look, 'heaven' in the first batch and 'seven' in the other! 'Heaven, seven'."

"Head of the class," King said. "Now take a look at the words for tiles Eight and Sixteen."

Leroy shook his head. "'Sea' rhymes with 'do-re-mi,' I suppose. But 'do-re-mi' seems an unlikely word to end a sentence. That's the last word, remember."

"Look at the tile again," Danforth said. "All the notes on the staff are quarter notes except the third one. It's a half note. And it's 'mi.' So what about Mr. Bishop just wanting the 'mi' to be used? Spelled with an 'e'?"

Leroy nodded. "Let's try it. 'Me', for the last word, Helen."

Helen wrote it down.

"Now," said Leroy, "if we use the words that rhyme for the end tiles, our first line would read: 'Left in mountain heaven.'"

"And the rest of the message comes out like this," Danforth said. "Left in mountain heaven Blank in blank sea Blank blank blank seven Blank blank in me."

"Clear as mud," Helen laughed. "All we have to do is fill in the blanks and somebody will inherit a tile-topped table."

Leroy was staring at the table top. "If it rhymes, maybe it's a short poem. And if it's a poem, it ought to scan."

"Modern poetry," Carol suggested, "doesn't scan once in a hundred times. That's effete and old-fashioned, didn't you know?"

"I refuse to acknowledge, even remotely, that Mr. Bishop might have been writing modern verse in tiles!" her husband reproved her. "He was a classicist, I'm sure. A teacher in Ravenna. So let's say, for the heck of it, that he intended his tile poem to scan. Where does that get us?"

"In deep trouble," Leroy said. "None of the words we thought of for tile Number Five is monosyllabic. And it would have to be—to scan like the first row of tiles."

"Suppose we use *part* of that first word under tile Number Five?" Carol said tentatively. "'Foundling' is obviously an accurate description of the picture. But just 'found' could describe it, too. A baby in a basket being 'found'—get it?"

"Sounds good," her husband said. "I only hope that doesn't mean Mr. Bishop was leaving a foundling to somebody in his will. That way lies madness. However, if we use 'found,' the second row of tiles reads: 'Found in opening sea.'"

"Wait, though, darling," Carol protested. "How come you used 'opening' for that third word?"

"It scans."

"And besides," Helen chimed in, "it would be silly to talk about a humpty-dumpty sea or a peek-a-boo sea or an aperture sea."

"This whole thing is nuts anyway," Carol said. "And there's something quite appealing to me about the phrase 'humpty-dumpty sea.' It speaks to me somehow. But I'll bow to the will of the majority— 'opening' it is. So we've got: "Left in mountain heaven Found in opening sea Quick blank blank seven—"

"Just a minute, Carol," King Danforth interrupted. "You said 'quick' for the first word in the third row of tiles. Why quick? The tile shows an oil lamp."

"I see why." Helen patted Carol's hand. "You're just a genius, darling, that's all. Certainly it's 'quick.' There's the wick in the lamp. And look at the odd shape of the lamp handle—that little handle-loop coming off to the right, it's shaped exactly like a Q. So 'Q' plus 'wick' spells 'quick'."

"I concede defeat," said Danforth with mock humility. "I guess you *are* pretty good at crossword puzzles at that."

"How about that next tile, though?" Leroy asked. "The teacup being emptied? Three of our descriptive words would scan there. We could have 'quick grounds,' 'quick dregs' or 'quick lees'."

Helen laughed. "Quick grounds seems to go more with coffee or divorce," she said, "than with a will."

Leroy was silent for an instant, holding up his hand dramatically. "Man," he said finally, "I think I've got hold of one from way out. Look. If the second tile in that row is 'lees' it makes a faintly familiar word when combined with the word ahead of it, 'quick.' The two together would read "quick lees'."

"An adverb if I ever heard one," said Carol. "But spelled wrong. Shouldn't have an 's' on the end."

"And it's never used any more in the singular," Danforth added, "that word 'lees'."

"Let me finish. What if the final 's' is a possessive? Then what do we get?"

"Something that belongs to quickly, whoever that is."

"Shakespeare!" Danforth cried. "Mistress Quickly! *Mary Wives of Windsor!*"

"Who else?" Leroy said smugly. "Who else ever had a name like that?"

"But why Mistress Quickly?" Helen argued. "What's she got to do with tile tables or Mr. Bishop's will?"

"Mistress Quickly," said Leroy, "if I remember correctly, was a servant to Doctor Caius in Shakespeare's play. She waited on him, served as his messenger, did his housekeeping, played hostess for him—"

"Ah!" Danforth nodded approvingly. "In a word, she was a kind of Mrs. Cardoni ? Because Mrs. Cardoni served in the same capacity for Mr. Bishop so faithfully? You think that Quickly in this rebus refers to Mrs. Cardoni?"

"Indubitably," said Leroy. "What do you think, girls?" They were staring at him with doubt plain on their faces.

"Well," said Helen with a kind of reluctant admiration, "you certainly reached for that one, darling. I suppose it could be."

"The verse ought to be easy from here on," Leroy proclaimed. "Which of the four words describing the next tile, Number Eleven, could belong to Mrs. Cardoni? 'Knight'—'sword'—'belt'—'gird'?"

"Ouch!" Helen said.

"Personally," said Danforth, "I find all of them slightly ludicrous when applied to our excellent landlady. Cardoni's knight? Not likely, however you spell 'knight.' Cardoni's sword? Huh-uh. Cardoni's belt? Well …"

"But how about the next one, King?" Carol asked. "Cardoni's 'gird.' Couldn't that be girdle?"

"Please!" said Leroy. "Mrs. Cardoni is amply favored above the waist, but her hips and waistline are quite trim. Girdle? It's unthinkable!"

"Hold it!" It was Danforth's turn to strike the pose of The Thinker. "I direct your attention to the tile itself. What is the man doing in the picture?"

"Putting on his sword."

"Yes. Now what's another way of saying 'put on' when one refers to a sword?"

"Arm," said Leroy. "Buckle on, clip on, gird on ..."

"Gird on," Danforth said, pleased. "Just the word. Gird on. Guerdon."

The girls regarded him blankly. "Are you sure that gimlet hasn't been too much for you?" Helen asked solicitously. "What's a 'guerdon'?—if I may exhibit my stupidity."

"A guerdon is a word less common now than formerly. But it means a reward."

"Oh!" Carol's lips moved as she read over to herself the message of the tiles with the new word addled. "So the third row of tiles reads: 'Quickly's guerdon seven'," she said aloud. "Seven what?"

Helen consulted her notes. "Seven 'cheerio, bye-bye, so long, or see you later.' I've heard of saying good bye several times, but seven farewells seems excessive."

"Tile Number Twelve is the only one with any leaves in it," Leroy said. "Those lovely, curving olive leaves are floating across the big figure Seven in the picture. Maybe Bishop wants us to notice the leaves."

"So—seven leaves. What's that mean?"

"Perhaps the rest of the tiles will tell us."

"All right. The first tile in the last row, Number Thirteen: a baby waving. 'Bye-bye' seems the logical choice."

"Or just 'by'," Helen suggested.

"Next," intoned Danforth, "we come to the final word—the one that rounds out this cryptic message. And it better be good. Because so far the whole thing makes as little sense as a series of undeciphered hieroglyphics."

"Maybe this last word will prove a Rosetta Stone," said Leroy smiling. "What's your fancy, ladies and gentleman? 'Seven leaves by song in me'? 'Seven leaves by music in me'? 'Seven leaves by hymn in me'? Or 'seven leaves by singing in me'?"

They all preferred 'hymn,' spelled 'him' since it was the only word that even approached intelligibility in its context.

"Now read the whole thing, Helen," Leroy directed.

"Left in mountain heaven
Found in opening sea
Quickly's guerdon seven
Leaves by him in me."

For a moment they were silent. Then Danforth sighed and shrugged and said gloomily, "Let's eat. It was a pleasant way to pass the time on a rainy afternoon. That's all I can say for it."

They went into the dining room. Helen, leading the way, was heard to murmur to Carol, "If our table in the dining room has a tile top, I'll scream!"

During the meal they chattered about everything but Mrs. Cardoni's tile coffee table. Nevertheless, from their preoccupied manner, Danforth and Leroy continued to think about it. When dinner was over, they moved into the lounge again for coffee. Mrs. Cardoni served it to them on Mr. Bishop's table.

"Listen," said Leroy when they were alone once more. "I hate to give up on this table rebus, don't you, King? It's a gorgeous puzzle."

"Who's giving up?" his partner said stoutly. "I needed to renew my strength with a few vitamins, that's all. I've been thinking. What about Bishop's background? We may find a clue there. What did he do in Ravenna? Teach?"

"Yes."

"All right." Danforth rubbed his cropped head. "What did he teach?"

"I'll find out." Leroy got up and went out into the small lobby of the hotel. Mrs. Cardoni was behind the desk, entering figures in a ledger. He said, "What was Mr. Bishop's specialty as a teacher in Ravenna, Mrs. Cardoni? Do you happen to know?"

"Of course," she replied. "Mr. Bishop was an authority on Italian literature."

"Thanks. That might prove helpful."

"Are you still trying to make sense out of those tiles?" she asked. "I'm really afraid you're wasting your time. The table is merely Mr. Bishop's legacy to me. It's all he had except the money I used to bury him with."

"You're probably right," Leroy said. He went back to the lounge and reported.

"Italian literature!" Danforth said, beaming. "That opens up a whole new field! Bishop ran to literary allusions apparently, judging from the Mistress Quickly bit. So maybe Italian literature holds the key."

"If there's any literature in the world I know nothing about," Carol said, "it's Italian. Let's play bridge."

Helen said, "I've read Dante's *Inferno*."

For an instant an electric silence held Danforth and Leroy. Then they began to speak simultaneously. Both stopped short. Then they grinned at each other—the familiar partnership grin they usually reserved for use when one of their complicated mystery plots had at last come right.

"Dante!" said Leroy.

"Dante!" echoed Danforth happily.

"Did I say something bright?" asked Helen. "If so, please explain it to me."

Martin Leroy said, "This may be the key, baby. You said you'd read Dante's *Inferno*. Have you ever read the entire *Divine Comedy*?"

"Not me. *Inferno* was more than enough for me, thank you."

Her husband went on. "The other two parts of the *Divine Comedy* are *Purgatory* and *Paradise*, and that's interesting, because the first line of tiles refers to 'heaven'—or paradise, if you prefer."

Danforth broke in. "Mart! Didn't Mrs. Cardoni say Bishop's name was Lemuel V. Bishop?"

"Yes?"

"Then the middle initial 'V' may be significant."

Leroy nodded. "Virgil!" he said. Their wives looked at them as though they had taken leave of their senses.

"Virgil!" said Helen. "I thought it was Dante."

"Don't you remember?" her husband asked blandly. "It was Virgil who guided Dante through Hell in the *Inferno*."

"Oh!"

Danforth said, "'Left in mountain heaven'—our first row of tiles. That means Virgil left Dante when they got to Paradise which was located at the top of the mountain of Purgatory, as I recall it. Because when they reached Paradise, the lovely Beatrice took over the guiding job from Virgil."

"And the second row of tiles!" Leroy almost shouted. "'Found in opening sea.' I'll give you three to one the 'sea' at the end of the row is supposed to be the letter 'C' and not an ocean. Get it?"

"Don't ask me," Carol said, "I never even read the *Inferno*!"

"It must stand for 'Canto'," Leroy said. "Virgil found Dante in the first part of the poem. In the opening Canto, as our verse says."

"So Virgil left Dante in heaven and found him in the first verse of the *Inferno*," Helen said. "Why should Bishop tell us that? That doesn't sound like part of a will."

"For identification purposes," Danforth said slowly. "To point to Dante as the 'him' of the tile verse. And to serve as a kind of signature to his will by calling attention to Virgil—if his middle name was really Virgil."

"It was," said Mrs. Cardoni, who had quietly come into the room behind them. She stood with her mouth slightly open, listening, her magnificent bosom visibly swelling and collapsing as she breathed.

"Okay," Leroy said. "Next: 'Quickly's reward seven'." Maddeningly, he broke off to grin at Mrs. Cardoni and interpolate, "That's you, Mrs. Cardoni. He calls you Mistress Quickly here in the tiles."

She merely stared at him.

"Quickly's guerdon seven," Danforth said. "Punctuate that properly and it makes more sense. Simply put a colon after 'guerdon'."

"Right. 'Quickly's guerdon—or reward: seven leaves by him in me'."

They all saw it at once.

"Leaves—*pages*!" Leroy cried.

"By Dante!" Helen said in awe.

"In me," Danforth finished, his tone expressing infinite satisfaction. "That must be the table. 'In me'. Not in Virgil, obviously. In the tile-topped table itself."

Mrs. Cardoni drew closer and stared with new fascination at the colorful tiles of the table top. "What does it mean, Mr. Leroy?" she asked in bewilderment.

"If it means what I think it means, you're going to inherit something pretty valuable."

"Valuable!" Danforth said. "Priceless is the word. Do you know something, my illiterate friends? Not a single manuscript page, not a line of handwriting, not one signature of Dante's has survived to our time. There just ain't any. So even if this should prove to be just seven printed pages of an early edition of great Dante's works, it will be priceless. And if it's actually part of the manuscript of the *Divine Comedy* ..."

Carol interrupted him. "Wait now, darling," she said earnestly. "Don't get Mrs. Cardoni's hopes up and then dash them. It's not fair. This whole thing is quite probably silly, Mrs. Cardoni. We've built up a message in the tiles from a crazy-quilt of words we selected quite arbitrarily, and then we've interpreted that message on the basis of clues so fragile as to be almost non-existent. You can see our chances of being right are just about a thousand to one."

"It *is* pretty far-fetched," her husband admitted. "But I honestly think we might—"

Carol interrupted him again. "All right. But why, if there *is* anything hidden under the tiles of the table, would Mr. Bishop have put it there in the first place, going to all this tile-painting and tablemaking trouble? Why not just hand it to Mrs. Cardoni and say, 'Here are some pages of Dante manuscript I want you to have when I die.'"

Leroy nodded. "A fair question, Carol. I think there may have been several reasons. First, I'm sure he must have been needling his lawyer brother just a bit in his quiet, scholarly way. He wanted to give this practical, serious-minded attorney a brand-new kind of will to decipher and file for probate! No doubt he gave his brother some cryptic clue to the reading of the tiles in his letter, so there would be no chance the message would *not* be read; but can you imagine his brother's embarrassment, carting this tile-topped table into the office of the register of wills or whatever it is, and trying to file it? Remember, Lemuel V. Bishop was presumably steeped in the literature and history of Italy, and to present his stuffy brother with a challenge of such Renaissance deviousness must have amused him."

"I must say it has delighted you," Carol smiled.

"The chief reason he did it," Danforth suggested, "was probably to protect Mrs. Cardoni's interests. Whatever's in the table, if it has anything to do with Dante, must be priceless, as I say. And Bishop didn't want Mrs. Cardoni, a babe in the woods in such a matter, to be cheated of her legacy's proper value if she should try to dispose of it herself. Bishop wanted his brother to handle it for her, so she'd be sure to get her rights."

Helen said, "You make it sound kind of convincing. But where, I can't help wondering, could Mr. Bishop have found anything like a Dante manuscript to begin with?'

"In Ravenna, probably," Danforth hazarded. "Dante was a political exile from Florence, his home town, for a long lime, you know. He died in Ravenna, I believe. So maybe Bishop had been rooting through dusty archives there most of his life, searching through old trunks in people's attics, and came across this treasure, whatever it is. Anyway, will you girls please stop with the questions and let us take this table apart? I am not a patient man, and Mrs. Cardoni is politely trying to keep from bursting with curiosity at this very moment." He smiled at the landlady who was indeed trembling with excitement. "Are you willing to let us commit mayhem on your table, Mrs. Cardoni?"

"For such a purpose, how can I refuse?"

"Good." Danforth turned the coffee table over so that its tiled top rested on the rug and its legs pointed toward the ceiling. The legs were screwed on individually. And there was no sign of any other screwhead on the plywood undersurface of the table. "We may have to break the tiles to get at those seven leaves," he said regretfully.

Leroy said, "Let's take the legs off first. Do you have a screwdriver handy, Mrs. Cardoni?"

She secured one from the hotel pantry in record time.

Leroy loosened the screws that held the table's tapered legs in place and removed them. Once the legs were off, four more screwheads appeared, one in each corner where the base of the leg had hidden it.

Helen, Carol, and Mrs. Cardoni leaned breathlessly over his shoulder as Leroy loosened these screws in turn. When the last screw came free, he inserted the tip of the screwdriver along the edge of the plywood and pried gently. The whole square of plywood came readily away.

They stared down at what lay between this false bottom, just removed, and the wooden base on which the tiles had been set.

Seven sheets of heavy, parchment-like vellum, yellowed with age and covered with spidery handwriting in faded brownish ink, stared back at them. Each sheet had been sealed by Lemuel V. Bishop into a transparent, damp-proof envelope of cellophane.

Mrs. Cardoni took a corset-creaking breath, speechless with astonishment. Impulsively, Carol put her arms around the landlady and hugged her. Leroy muttered, "Seven leaves, by Jove!"

But Danforth said in a disappointed, puzzled voice, "But that's Latin, not Italian vernacular! It can't be part of the *Divine Comedy* manuscript!"

He leaned down over Leroy's shoulder and delicately, with his fingertips, moved aside several of the sheets that overlapped others, revealing the lower portion of sheet Number Seven—the one that had been hidden underneath. "Look!" he breathed. "Latin, Italian, or Sanskrit—what's the difference? Do you see what that is?"

They followed his pointing finger with their eyes. They saw the two words, unmistakably clear and unblurred even through the cellophane, and written in the same spidery script as the rest: *Dante Aligh-ieri.*

"His signature!" Danforth said. "As sure as his own Hell!" He looked up into Mrs. Cardoni's face. "Mrs. Cardoni," he said solemnly, "if that is an authentic signature, you can change your name to Mrs. Croesus."

* * * *

The *Valhalla* left Naples the following afternoon for Piraeus. The Danforths and Leroys were aboard to continue their cruise around the world. They had personally committed Mrs. Cardoni and her seven "leaves" to the scholarly ministrations of the Director of the Naples *Biblioteca*, a man named Pietro Carlo who providentially turned out to be distantly related to her dead husband's family. He had promised faithfully to look after Mrs. Cardoni's interests in the matter of the manuscript pages as well as to advise them just what her legacy consisted of when he should have settled that controversial question.

But it was not until the unbelievable beauty of Greece lay behind them and the *Valhalla* was making for Port Said and the Suez Canal at a steady twenty knots that they heard the final word on their Positano adventure.

They were having dinner when a steward brought Danforth a radiogram. He tore it open. "It's from Carlo, in Naples," he said, and proceeded to read its contents aloud:

> Happy to report your find seems authentic. Evidently fragment of rough draft of letter written in Latin by Dante to his most illustrious protector while in exile, Can Grande della Scala of Verona, immortalized in 17th Canto of *Paradisio*. Letter is famous, containing directions for interpreting *Divina Commedia*. This rough draft conforms in most respects with accepted text of that letter, of which original mss., along with all other Dante mss., has been lost. Signature alone worth millions. But Mrs. Cardoni has agreed to make a gift of legacy to Italy, provided it be officially designated as Lemuel V. Bishop-Leroy King Collection in National Library. She asks me convey her respects and deep thanks for your help. Also assurance of free lodgings at Savoia Hotel any future visits you make to Positano.
> Pietro Carlo

P.S. Italy thanks you, too.

They were silent when he finished reading. At length Danforth called the wine steward to their table and ordered champagne. When it was poured, he lifted his glass. "I'd like to propose a toast," he said, "a double toast."

"Hear! Hear!" said Helen.

"First," said Danforth, "to Mrs. Cardoni, a gracious, great-hearted lady who richly deserved her good fortune but chose to give it up for patriotic and generous reasons."

"Mrs. Cardoni!" they all said, and drank.

"And second," continued Danforth, "let's drink to Leroy King and his charming wives who, though nothing but humble writers of detective fiction, have managed for once in their lives to give some genuinely great literature to the world!"

They drained their glasses.

JAMES HOLDING (1907-1997) was a prolific author primarily of short stories, but also of children's picture-books and young adult mysteries such as the "Ellery Queen, Jr." novels, which he ghost-wrote.

Holding was, by all reports, a bright, ambitious, energetic youth. He attended Yale University, where he was a member of the Alpha Chi Rho fraternity, and graduated with an A.B. in 1928. After graduation, he spent a year exploring Europe. When he returned home, he took a sales job, but soon found a more creative calling in advertising as junior copywriter for the ad company Batte, Barton, Durstine & Osborne in Pittsburgh. In 1931, he married Janet Spice, with whom he had two children, James C.C. Holding III (1933-2010) and Donald Angus Holding (1937-1953).

His career in advertizing proved successful. He rose swiftly in the ranks to copywriter, then in 1944 became copy chief. He created such advertising slogans as "Fort Pitt, That's It!" for Fort Pitt Beer. In 1952, he became vice-president of BBD&O.

Tragedy struck in 1953, with the death of his second son, Donald, in a beach accident while vacationing in Canada. The boy was only 16. James Holding took it hard, and it affected his advertising work. Ultimately he stepped down as Vice President from BBD&O (though he would remain as a consultant for the next decade). Instead, he focused his attention on a lifelong dream—a career as a writer. He set about it with the same drive and determination which made him a successful advertising executive, and the results of his labors were immediate: 1959 saw the sales of his first nine short stories, starting with "An Accident in Honiaria," which appeared in *Alfred Hitchcock's Mystery Magazine*, and "The Treasure of Pachacamac," which appeared in *Ellery Queen's Mystery Magazine* (both published in June 1960). He also cracked the lucrative children's picture-book market in 1962. More than 250 short stories and poems and 20 children's books would follow.

Mystery stories remained his forté when writing for adults. He published prolifically in all the leading magazines of the day.

In early 2015, Wildside Press purchased James Holding's copyrights from his daughter-in-law and has been working to reissue his work. A complete collection of the "Leroy King" series is forthcoming from Crippen & Landru in 2017.

BESIDE A FLOWERING WALL

Fletcher Flora

Originally published in *Alfred Hitchcock's
Mystery Magazine*, April 1968.

Having become a creature of habit, the stale protagonist of a domestic regimen, Ruth awoke that morning, as usual, at almost precisely
eight o'clock. The odd thing about her regimen, including the precision
schedule of waking, was that it was, and had been from the beginning,
entirely unnecessary. So far as her commitments were concerned, her
obligation to be here or there at this hour or that, she might as well
have awakened anytime and at her discretion have gone anywhere.

Yet, commitments aside, the regimen was, for its own reasons, essential. It gave order and stability to a life that would have, without
it, blown apart in an explosion of centrifugal pressure or, even worse,
have diminished and died in the dust of abandoned hopes and sustained frustration. She was, indeed, like the compulsive alcoholic who
must adhere to the discipline of abstinence or submit to the anarchy
of excess.

This particular morning, however, although it began for her at the
time and in the place of other mornings, was in fact the morning of
such a day as she had never lived and would never live again. It was, in
prospect, the culmination of all the years of days that had gone before
it, and it would be, before it was over, the end of them. It would be,
by the terms of a kind of destined and dreadful rationale, the end of
all that had never been done, the suffix of all that had never been said.

She had planned the day, insofar as she was able, quite carefully.
It was characteristic of her, as she had become, that even her aberra-
tions, the willful departure from accustomed ways and normal expectations, must somehow sustain the quality of habit, every strange effect
of every disturbing cause somehow anticipated and rehearsed, as if she
would otherwise be lost and impotent in a confusion of wanton reac-
tions. The planning had begun, in fact, late in the afternoon of the day

before; a few minutes after five o'clock, to be as precise as possible.

Ruth always had two very dry martinis at five o'clock, or rather in the half hour following the hour, and Mrs. Groat, who came in days to clean and cook, had just brought in the little silver tray with the silver shaker and the delicate long-stemmed glass of shining crystal. The telephone in the hall had begun to ring at that instant, and Mrs. Groat had gone to answer it, leaving Ruth to pour the first martini for herself, in itself a deviation from the normal that now seemed, in retrospect, to be darkly prophetic. Ruth had just taken her first sip from the delicate glass, when Mrs. Groat returned with news that was, if not revolutionary, at least unusual enough to excite her curiosity. "Someone for you," Mrs. Groat said. "A man."

Ruth had experienced no sudden and mysterious intuition about the call. After all, she was still called occasionally by men, almost invariably on matters of business, and there was no reason why she should have expected this particular call to be in any way unusual. Putting her glass on the little table beside her chair, she went past Mrs. Groat into the hall, picked up the phone and said, "Hello."

"Ruth?" the man's voice queried.

Then, of course, she knew. The single syllable of her name was spoken as casually as if it prefaced a response to something she had said a decade ago, and she stood mute for a moment, her brain scalded with remembrance. After the mute moment, because it was imposed by a fierce pride, she answered with a voice that was miraculously contained "Yes. Who's speaking, please?"

"It's Pat. Pat Brady."

"Pat!" She permitted an inflection of surprise to enter her voice. "Where in the world are you?"

"I'm in St. Louis."

She had assumed that the call was local, and she felt an irrational anger at the electronic marvel of direct long-distance dialing. Previously, you would at least have had the intermediate operator to warn you of the unexpected, so that you would have an instant to prepare the reaction of pleasure or excitement or shock, or to disguise, as she was disguising now, the sickening ambivalence incited by what had been and what was.

"That's too bad," she said. "I'd enjoy seeing you again."

"That's why I called. I'm at loose ends tomorrow, and I'd like to see you again, too. Would it be convenient if I came? I'd have only a couple of hours in town at the most."

"Are you sure you want to come all the way from St. Louis for just a couple of hours?"

"Nothing to it. I'll hop a jet in the morning and be there in a flash. I'll take another jet out in the afternoon."

"What time should I expect you?"

"You name the hour, and I'll be on your doorstep."

"Would two o'clock in the afternoon be all right?"

"Fine. Expect me then. Same old place?"

"Same old place. Mother and Father are both dead now. Perhaps you'd heard."

"I hadn't. I'm sorry."

"Well, one adjusts after a while."

"Of course. Nothing else to do. Until tomorrow then, Ruth."

"Until tomorrow. Good-bye, Pat."

It was miraculous, truly miraculous, how calmly she had spoken his name. She was exorbitantly proud of herself, of her miraculous control. To demonstrate to herself that it was secure, not just something she had achieved briefly by a great effort, she repeated the name three times to herself with a kind of deliberate and lilting cadence: *Pat, Pat, Pat*. She cradled the telephone and returned to the living room where Mrs. Groat, who had eavesdropped, was clearly torn between an uncertain respect for Ruth's privacy and her own agitated curiosity. Leaning toward the latter, she hovered in hope. Ruth, aware of this, sat down in her chair and picked up her glass from the silver tray. How steady her hand was! The glass, on its way to her lips, did not shake in the least. Not a drop of the precious pale liquid was lost from it. And how good the strong martini was! It slipped smoothly down her throat and gathered in her stomach in a warm little puddle.

"That was an old friend," she said. "I knew him quite well a long time ago. His name is Pat Brady."

"How nice." Mrs. Groat, whose experience with men had confirmed her mother's warnings, sounded vaguely belligerent. "Will he be coming to call?"

"Yes. Tomorrow afternoon."

"Will you want me to prepare something special? Tea or early cocktails or something?"

"No, thank you. As a matter of fact, you may plan to have the afternoon off. Pat and I will have so many things to catch up on. We'll manage quite well, I'm sure."

Mrs. Groat's open face suddenly closed. Uncertain whether she should rejoice in her unexpected half-holiday or take offense at what might be her peremptory exclusion, she retreated to the kitchen to analyze the development.

Ruth, lifting her glass to her lips again, discovered with a slight shock that it was empty. She had drunk the martini much too fast. Really, she must try to restrain herself. Two martinis between five and five-thirty were her quota, her absolute limit except on those rare occasions that might be called special, and she always paced her consumption of them to last the full half-hour. Having drunk one already, at barely ten minutes after the hour, she would simply have to pace more slowly for the next twenty minutes. Or could this occasion, perhaps, be called special? Well, hardly. Tomorrow, however, was another matter. Tomorrow would be special. Tomorrow she would have her martinis earlier, and it was entirely possible, even probable, that she would have three, or even four.

Already she was making plans. In fact, although she was not consciously aware of it, she had begun planning the moment she cradled the telephone. That was evidenced by her prompt and rather ruthless exclusion of Mrs. Groat, who would only be in the way. Threes a crowd, Mrs. Groat. Extras are unwelcome on special occasions, Mrs. Groat. So sorry, Mrs. Groat, but you are not wanted.

She emptied the silver shaker into the delicate crystal glass and took the first sip of her second martini in her disciplined drinking. She was tempted by her growing excitement to drink with reckless haste, but she managed, by a stern exercise of will, to stretch the martini over the remaining twenty minutes, and it was just five-thirty when she got down to what would have been the olive if she ordinarily bothered with olives, which she did only on special occasions. Like tomorrow, for example; tomorrow she would have olives.

Leaving her glass beside the shaker on the tray, Ruth went upstairs to her room. The room was large and light, at the front of the house. It had once been the room of her parents, but now her parents were dead; dead and buried side by side in the cemetery east of town, and the room was hers. She crossed the room to a window overlooking the front yard and stood staring out across the yard and the street to the house directly opposite. In other years there had been no house there, only a beloved and beautiful vacant lot, beaten bare by the neighborhood kids who had gathered to play baseball and shinny on fair days, and Pump, Pump, Pull Away in the soft interminable dusks of summer. Next to the house that now stood where the lot had been, was the house in which Pat had been born and had lived out the years of his boyhood. Shifting the direction of her gaze, looking across the street obliquely, she could see the house.

Oh, he had been a beautiful boy! Swift and strong he had been, and good at games, and later adept in love. It was no wonder she had loved him desperately all those years. The wonder was that he had loved her, for she had been a plain girl, as she was a plain woman, with an odd faded look as if she had been laundered too many times in boiling water. Of course, a girl's looks are not important to a boy when he is very young. What is important is her steadfast loyalty and her readiness to do what a young boy wants to do. And he *had* loved her. He *had*. His love had survived puberty, and the years after, and it had survived in the after-years the trials of abortive expression in this private place or that, at one fearful and ecstatic time or another.

Then, in the end, it had come to nothing. That was the shame of it, the terrible degradation. If only it had ended, if it had to end, in an explosion of fury or a flash of tragedy. If only it had ended in a way that was worthy of the quality of her love—but it hadn't. Instead, it had expired with a whimper. For him, it had died of apathy. It had simply come to *nothing*.

Turning away from the window, she went into the bathroom. In the mirror above the lavatory, she saw the reflection of her face and paused deliberately to study it dispassionately. Her face was another shameful thing. It was not so much that she minded being plain, or even ugly. She would have preferred, in fact, a distinctive ugliness. What she minded was the faded effect of anemia—the *nothingness*. It was a lie, that's what it was. Her face was a *lie*. It denied the fierce intensity of her heart and brain. It obscured the history of her total commitment to love in her early years, and of her love's cruel mutation in the desolate years afterward.

She evaded the lie by opening the medicine cabinet door. Reaching behind a screen of bottles on the top shelf, she removed a small box. There was no label on the lid of the box. Removing the lid, she stood staring at the white powder the box contained. She could not recall the name of the powder, and made no effort to do so, but she knew well enough its potential. In her hand, in the small box, she was holding sudden death for at least a dozen people. Her father had been a pharmacist and a successful businessman. He had owned three drugstores when he died, two years after her mother's death, and she had gone the day after his funeral to one of the stores, which had since been sold, and had taken this powder from behind the prescription counter. In the bleak newness of being utterly alone she had thought she would like to die. It was not that she had loved her parents so much, or that she even missed them excessively for themselves when they were gone. It was just the loneliness. If she had married Pat, as she had expected and planned, the death of her father would have meant little more to her than a minor adjustment and a large inheritance.

Anyhow, she had decided not to die; not yet. As she had once lived for her only love, she continued to live for the love's mutation. The day would come, would surely come, when she would have the chance to make right what had all these years been wrong. If she could not recover the love, she could at least remove its shame. She could give to her love, the truth in her heart behind the lie in her face, the proud and star-crossed ending it deserved.

Staring at the snowy powder in the little box, she formed with her lips the shape of a word: *Tomorrow*.

* * * *

Today—today was yesterday's tomorrow—and now that it had begun, it was necessary to get through it, from minute to minute and hour to hour, until it was spent, ended, at whatever time the ending came. Ruth got out of bed and showered and dressed in sweater and slacks, and then she sat down in front of her dressing table and began to brush her light brown hair a hundred strokes. Her head, canted first this way and then that, according to which side of the part she was brushing on, and when she had finished the hundred strokes exactly, fifty on each side of the part, she laid the brush on the table, avoiding her image in the mirror, and went out into the hall. With the door closed behind her, she could hear Mrs. Groat, who carried a key to the back door, at her work in the kitchen below. Mrs. Groat was a noisy worker, seeming to *attack* every task as if she feared a counterattack, and it was a constant wonder to Ruth that she did not leave behind her a litter of damaged pots and shattered glass and china. Even the vacuum sweeper, operated by Mrs. Groat, assumed a kind of roar, as if it were powered by a miniature jet engine.

Having descended the stairs, Ruth found her place set as usual on the table in the dining room, the electric percolator giving off the good, rich smell of coffee on the server near at hand. She poured a cup of coffee and sat down at her place, and Mrs. Groat, hearing her arrive on her usual schedule on this unusual day, came in from the kitchen with a glass of orange juice.

"Good morning," Mrs. Groat said.

"Good morning."

Ruth, leaning slightly forward over her cup, inhaled the rich vapors. Mrs. Groat lingered, sensing the day's difference and anticipating some kind of minor revolution.

"The usual breakfast?" Mrs. Groat asked, her voice brusque.

"Yes," Ruth said. "The usual" The usual, in addition to coffee and juice, was one slice of buttered toast, two strips of crisp bacon, and one egg over easy. Mrs. Groat, vaguely disappointed in the failure of revolution to develop, returned to the kitchen, and Ruth began to drink her steaming coffee. She had just finished the cupful when Mrs. Groat came back with her plate. Ruth was, surprisingly, quite hungry. The excitement within her, contained and growing, nourished by her expectations, had given an edge to her appetites and senses.

She finished her breakfast, and then, because it was a fair day, and because she was too large for the house with the excitement growing and growing within her, she went out into the yard and cut flowers and brought them in and arranged them in a vase, which she placed in the living room. Then she went back out into the yard and pruned and dug and watered and did a dozen things that did not need doing at all, or could have been done later, because it was essential, absolutely essential, that the hours of the morning be filled, the time passed, and somehow the hours were and time was.

At noon, she went back into the house and washed her hands and face and had her lunch and went upstairs to her room. She lay down on her bed, neatly made by Mrs. Groat, and she wished that she could sleep, could close her eyes and know nothing and open them again just in time to do what must be done before it was too late for doing anything. It was, of course, impossible to sleep with her excitement now monstrous and pulsing and scarcely containable, and it would hardly have been worthwhile anyhow, even if it had been possible, because Mrs. Groat clumped upstairs just before one o'clock and knocked on the door and came in uninvited. She was wearing her hat with an effect of belligerence, and she was clutching her purse like a primitive weapon.

"If you have no further use for me," she said, "I'll be leaving now."

She made it sound as if, after faithful service, she were being discarded. Ruth sat up on the edge of the bed. She wondered if Mrs. Groat could sense her excitement, could feel it in the air or hear it in her voice or see it seeping through her skin like a vapor, and it seemed incredible that Mrs. Groat could not.

"That's fine," Ruth said. "Enjoy your afternoon."

"Thank you." Mrs. Groat did not sound optimistic. "I'll see you in the morning."

"Yes, as usual. In the morning."

Ruth pronounced the word with no sense of reality. A word is what it was. Morning was a word, a sound, without substance or prospects. What was real, real and here and suddenly demanding, was this afternoon, two o'clock this afternoon, and now she would have to hurry, having waited so long, to do in advance what needed doing. She undressed and took another shower and stood for a minute or two in front of the long mirror on the inside of the bathroom door to look at her lean body, so much more beautiful than her shameful nothing face, and she felt all at once a great pity and regret for the terrible waste of her beautiful lean body. In the bedroom she dressed carefully, putting on at last a pale green sleeveless sheath. By that time it was one-thirty, a little past, and she went back into the bathroom and took the small box of powder from the medicine cabinet and carried it downstairs. In the kitchen she made a shaker of martinis and put the shaker in the freezer compartment of the refrigerator. When martinis got crackling cold, she had discovered, they became just slightly thick and exceptionally good. Next, she set the silver tray on the cabinet beside the sink and placed on the tray a small bowl of olives and a pair of crystal glasses. Beside the tray she placed the small box of powder.

It will only require a little, *she thought*. A pinch apiece for the two crystal glasses.

The thought did not depress her. On the contrary, it was exhilarating, a lyric expression of her sustained excitement. The exhilaration cried out for accompaniment. Turning away, she went into the living room and looked among the recordings in the cabinet of her stereophonic phonograph. There! That was just right. That was just what she needed, what her mood needed, at once gay and grave and exalted. She put the recording on the phonograph and stood listening to the first movement of Mozart's Jupiter symphony, and the first movement ended, and the second movement began, and then, halfway through the second movement, the front doorbell rang.

How assured she was! How fully in control of the terrible excitement that tried to rise from her breast into her throat and strangle her! She was proud of her assurance, her quiet command of her furious heart. Leaving the Jupiter to play itself out, she walked into the hall and opened the door. At that instant, as the door opened and she saw the man standing outside with his hat in his hands at the far end of a decade gone, her mind was trespassed by a scrap of verse, a strange and perverse lyric culled from a litter of odds and ends for some reason remembered:

I saw my dear, the other day,
Beside a flowering wall;
And this was all I had to say:
"I thought that he was tall!"

How many years ago had she read that? Oh, years and years, in a book of poems by Dorothy Parker. But why had it lain intact and dormant so long in her mind to be remembered at this instant? Was it just that the man outside her door seemed in the instant, whatever he had been and still was, somehow deficient? That was nonsense. The deficiency was not in him, but in her immediate *response* to him, because her anticipation and excitement had tricked her into expecting too much too soon. Closing her eyes, she saw him suddenly, at once reduced and enlarged, growing in a vision from a boy to a man, and her contained excitement was restored with the vision.

"Pat," she said "How nice to see you again."

"Hello, Ruth. You look the same as ever."

"You know better. I'm ten years older, and I'm sure I show them all. Come in, Pat. We have so much to say to each other."

He left his hat in the hall and followed her into the living room. The Jupiter was still playing. She turned it down and sat beside him on the sofa, the interval between them suggesting to her the separation by scale, as on a map, of what they had been and what they were.

"I'm afraid I won't be able to stay as long as I hoped," he said. "An hour at the longest. My schedule's tighter than I thought, and it will take me the better part of an hour to get back to the airport."

Small matter, *she thought*. It will be better to end quickly, now that the time is here, what has taken far too long already.

"Then you must tell me all about yourself at once," she said.

"There isn't much to tell." His voice struck a note of false humility which she felt uneasily was a kind of inverted pretension. He was too well preserved, too immaculately groomed, even after a long taxi ride, in clothes that were too obviously expensive. "After college, you remember, I went to San Francisco. After a year I dropped down to Los Angeles, and I've been there ever since."

"I didn't know. I've had no word from you all this time."

"I'm sorry. I intended to keep in touch, but you know how these things are. A man gets involved, he doesn't have much time for old friends and places."

"I must say that you seem to have done very well," Ruth said.

"I've been able to get my share, I guess."

"What do you do?"

"I'm in real estate. Real estate and insurance."

"Oh? You used to want to paint. We used to talk about it."

He laughed, and she listened intently with fierce longing for a suggestion of wistfulness in the sound, the merest whisper of sadness for old hope abandoned and limitations enduring—but there was none. His laughter was brief and untroubled, an expression of indifference tainted with disdain.

"I soon had that fantasy knocked out of my head, once I was out on my own. Business is the thing for me. There's where you're up against the real competition. There's where you find the men with drive and vision. Believe me, you have to stay alert if you hope to stay up front."

"Are you up front?"

"Well, I don't like to blow my own horn, you know, but I manage to hold my own. Maybe I've had some luck, too. You have to get a few breaks as you go along. Still, in the long run, you make your own breaks. The secret is in cultivating the right people. Profitable associations, you know. I've been put next to some great opportunities by men in position to do me a good turn, not by chance."

"I'm delighted. I've often wondered what you were doing. It's comforting to know that you have done well."

"Oh, never worry about old Pat. I have a way of taking care of myself. Right now, as a matter of fact, I've got a show on the road that stands to make me a mint. Would you like to hear about it?"

"Please tell me. You can't imagine how fascinated I am."

"Nothing to it, as I implied, if you know a few people in the right places. I was handed a bit of advance information, very confidential, that a certain area is due for fast promotion and development, a kind of crash program I was able to get in on the ground floor; to buy up a big tract of land at a very good price, you understand. Next month I start building. Modern, medium-priced houses, a classy little residential area with a lot of eye-appeal, you know; variety of construction, nice landscaping and a community club and pool—all that. It represents a big investment, but it'll pay big dividends. You wait and see."

"I hardly can. You must let me know immediately."

"Yes, sir! Business is the thing. Old Silent Cal was dead right years ago. The business of this country is business. He was before our time, of course, but I remember reading that remark. I think I've got it right. Didn't Calvin Coolidge say that?"

"I don't know. I read so little about Calvin Coolidge."

"If you're interested in my opinion, he was a great man, a great president. He was smart enough to put first things first and then leave them alone. There's too much meddling nowadays by the government—all these left-wing fellows. That's the trouble with most of your writers and artists and professors—so-called intellectuals, radicals, people like that. They'll wreck the country if they aren't stopped."

"Perhaps it won't matter in the end. Perhaps all together we will wreck the whole world, and then nothing else will matter."

"What? Oh, you mean The Bomb. In my judgment, there's far too much loose talk about that. What we'd better be worrying about is all this creeping socialism that's taking over everything. But you don't want to get me started on that subject. I might forget the time and miss my jet."

"Yes. You mustn't forget your jet."

"Right." He shot a sleeve and looked at his watch. "Plenty of time however. How did we get started on business and politics, anyhow? We ought to be talking old times. I passed one of your father's old drugstores downtown. It's changed names."

"After my father died I sold the stores."

"You shouldn't have done it. You should have run them yourself. A clever woman like you could have done wonders with them; branched out in other towns, developed a chain."

"I am not a pharmacist."

"No matter. You can hire pharmacists by the dozen. Your father was realistic enough to understand that."

"I was not interested. Perhaps I have no drive or vision."

"Too bad. Do you live alone here?"

"Yes. Alone."

"You haven't changed things much."

"Very little. Are your parents well?"

"Father's dead. Mother's still around. Quite a problem sometimes, Mother is."

"Does she live with you?"

"Hardly. Living with Mother would be impossible. Evelyn and I agreed on that before we were married. Families don't mix."

"You're married? I didn't know."

"Wrong tense. *Was* married. It didn't work, and it didn't last long. Couple of years. Since then, I've carefully preserved my independence."

She thought of something then, a possibility that she had not considered before, and she couldn't for the life of her understand why she had not.

"Do you have children? A child?"

"Fortunately, no. Evelyn saw to that, I'm happy to say. It was, I believe, the only sane position she ever took on anything."

"You sound as if your marriage was unhappy. I'm sorry."

"Don't be. It was a mistake from the beginning, a sick sort of joke, and I was lucky to get out of it. How about you? Have you made the big mistake?"

"I've made mistakes, but not that one. I haven't married."

"Remember when we were kids? *We* were going to get married someday. Remember?"

"I remember."

"Well, things change; plans and people and things. As I came down the block I saw that the old vacant lot across the street is gone. We had great times on that lot."

"Yes. Great times."

So he came to them at last, after real estate and insurance and creeping socialism and birth control and divorce and Calvin Coolidge. The great times. The early days, the sweet, fierce days of total commitment before the mutated bitter aftermath—his voice went on and on, assaulting the fragile past, evoking and evading the holy places of their adolescent intimacy, and she sat and listened mutely in the cold and arid climate of her private wasteland. She was drained of pride and soiled with shame. She was dying, dying. She was a religious dying in the terrible conviction that there was, after all, no God. Fool that she was, she had wasted her love, and her hate after her love, on an absurd lie.

Why couldn't he have become a magnificent failure or a fanatic or even a splendid rogue? *The wild, silent crying of her mind was her elegy and his epitaph.* Why couldn't he have become anything but a bore?

He looked again at his watch, and she was, she discovered, suddenly standing.

"It must be almost time for you to leave," she said. "I have martinis made. Will you have one before you go?"

"Thanks," he said. "One for the road. I'll just call a taxi while you're getting it."

She went into the kitchen and removed the shaker from the freezer. She poured martinis into the two delicate crystal glasses on the silver tray. She dropped olives into the glasses and took up the small box of powder. For a moment she held it in both hands below her breasts in what was almost a gesture of love, and then she threw it with a gesture of violence across the kitchen. The box struck a cabinet on the opposite side and fell to the floor. The lid flew off, and the powder spread like a skim of snow on the bright tile. Lifting the silver tray, she carried it into the living room.

"They are quite dry," she said. "I like my martinis quite dry."

He took a glass, and she, after placing the tray on a table, lifted her own.

"Old times," he said.

"Yes. Old times."

The horn of the taxi sounded as they finished drinking, and she walked with him to the front door, but she did not linger to watch him go down to the street where the taxi was waiting. When he paused once to turn and wave, the door was closed and she was gone.

In the living room, sitting on the sofa, she drank slowly over a period of half an hour the three martinis that were left in the shaker.

I'm free, *she thought*. Now I am free.

In the terrifying emptiness of her freedom, with nothing left to live for and nothing worth dying for, she sat and drank the martinis.

✗

Fletcher Flora (1914-1968) was born in Kansas and educated at the University of Kansas, Lawrence. He served in the Army during WW2 and rose to the rank of Sergeant. He married Betty Ogden in 1940 and in 1945 was appointed Education Adviser to the Department of the Army, a position he held till 1963. He wrote or co-wrote sixteen novels under his own name plus three as "Ellery Queen." His short stories appeared in all the leading mystery magazines of the day.